John Earnest:
A Model Hydroplane Legend

by

Dianne Earnest

A Model Hydroplane Legend

Earnest Acres Publishers USA

John Earnest: A Model Hydroplane Legend

Case ID: 1-14934834251

Paperback - 978-1-967178-97-1

Publisher: Earnest Acres Publishers

Contact: dianneearnest@yahoo.com

This is a biographical work. Disclaimer: If some stories or descriptions appear slightly exaggerated or less than precise, you may be right.

Printed in the United States of America

DEDICATION

For John

The most encouraging, skilled model hydroplane builder I have ever met, dedicated to the sport he loves—and the love of my life.

FOREWORD

John Earnest will be most remembered for his boat-building skills, his love of model hydroplane racing, and his fierce competitive spirit. His unassuming, friendly attitude and dry sense of humor represent the hobby of model hydroplane racing at its finest. He is always willing and eager to talk about the sport.

He has made high-quality boats using only top-grade materials since 1973.

He has always used the best designs and has learned from the best builders. He has a vast knowledge of building and racing boats. Many racers have spent hours in John's workshop receiving knowledge and assistance with their own boats. He demonstrates that this sport is a hobby and that developing friendships and camaraderie each season are as important as racing boats.

John does not try to be showy, loud, or flashy. He is, however, consistent, always aiming at the whole season, not just at the next heat. Ever aware of other racers' commitment in time, energy, and money spent, John has, by choice, finished second or third so that boat racers don't have to go home with their boats in a bag.

John's love of the hobby, attention to detail, years on the scale hydro racing circuit, and honest concern for his fellow competitors have made him a legend in his own time.

John's Boat Gale V U-55

ACKNOWLEDGEMENTS

Harry Collier, Roger Newton, Les Ruggles, John Howell, Brian Buaas, Brad Lewis, Skip Young, and all those who helped John learn about the sport and who helped refine his skills.

Patrick Brown, Dallas Cook, and Ezra Kidowski for encouragement in writing this book. Rose City Model Yacht Club Collection of historic information from Dallas Cook Radio Control Unlimited Club Electric Radio Control Unlimited Club Hydroplane and Race Boat Museum in Kent, Washington

TABLE OF CONTENTS

CHAPTER ONE
IN THE BEGINNING...

Long before John became a hydroplane legend, he was a baby boy growing up in a country at war. His childhood was filled with stories—some heroic, some hilarious, and some passed down so often they became family lore. One of the earliest began with a frantic cry: "Robert! Where have you left John?!"

Robert was just coming to the realization that Ida was crying out to him in alarm and trying to recall where he had put John. The baby was only 6 months old, born on April 10, 1943. First time Grandma Ide (Ida) had asked Grandpa Robert, a new-time grandpa, to watch John while she finished the canning and started supper. The following is the story John heard many times as he was growing up.

"Grampe (Grandpa Robert) forgot John down with the rotting meat and the rats. Mom was upset, too." As John recalls, "Grampe really liked me and would take me downstairs when he was feeding the dogs. Downstairs was a hand-poured cement basement. An outside stairwell out the back door, under the bathroom window. Framed window casings with metal grids to keep out the larger varmints sufficed to allow air and light in the dank, unheated cellar. A woodpile was near the stairs to keep the wood dry and handy for supplying the great central fireplace at the home's entrance and for the cooking stove in the kitchen. A ringer washer was to one side and a few lines for hanging clothes when the Bothell, Washington, rains made outside drying impossible. In another part of the basement was a substantial table that held open boxes of meat, leftover from the butcher shops, ready to be mixed with meal for feeding the dogs. These boxes attracted flies and rats alike.

Grampe was proud of his new title, being a grandfather for the first time. He was also proud of his prize-winning hunting dogs. He had gone to the basement with the baby to cut up the meat, mix it with dog food, then take the mash to the crazed dogs in the shed out in the backyard. They were barking and milling in anticipation of the frenzied feeding which Robert knew would ensue. His reasoning was probably, "John will be safe and spared from the racket of the four dogs at feeding time." Having finished his chores with filling the water trough and feeding the chickens, he had completely forgotten the baby propped up against the woodpile downstairs in the basement.

As he entered the kitchen, Robert was startled out of his reverie at his wife's sharp cry asking WHERE WAS JOHN?! Grampe retraced his steps to the basement with a quicker step than usual to retrieve little John. The six-month-old was still contentedly gumming away, drool dripping down his bib and shirt. His teething toy was a converted duck bill, a natural choice for a child in a household of bird hunters. That night, John remained safe in his mother's arms, unaware of the chaos he'd caused. It was just the beginning of a childhood shaped by war, movement, and the steady love of family.

WORLD WAR II BEGINS

By fall of 1943, the world was no longer a stable place. The war had grown into a global conflict, and like many American families, the Earnests found their lives upended. Dictators had sprung up, rumors of concentration camps, and dreadful battles and bombings were daily newscasts on the radio.

John's mother and father had married in 1940, and by 1943, when his father joined the Navy, the Second World War was well underway. When boot camp was over, his dad was assigned to an LST—in Navy jargon, Large Slow Target—on the Atlantic front, shuttling much-needed food and supplies to England.

His mom had a job at the Smith Tower in Seattle. A new building, it housed the Fish and Game Department, where she was hired as a secretary. John's dad, Don Earnest, had hired on first, since his degree was in Fish Biology. It was a good fit, but then the war came.

John Robert Earnest, the model hydroplane legend, was born on April 10, 1943, in Seattle, Washington. It was a happy coincidence that he was born in Seattle, often referred to as the birthplace of hydroplane racing out west. He was near hydros from the very beginning. Since his grandfather, Robert Earnest, was a wood shop teacher for many years in the Seattle Public Schools, it was only natural that John's first boats were wooden hydroplanes.

In 1943, plans changed drastically for the new little family. His father was off to the war. Zona still needed to work. It was decided if she lived with Don's parents in Bothell, who had an extra bedroom, then Ida could watch baby John while Zona could commute to Seattle with Grampe Robert in the mornings and come home in the evenings. It made the commute handy. This arrangement lasted for about a year and worked well.

Ida Marie Hollan Earnest was delighted at the prospect. Care and feeding were left to her. Meme Ide was her enviable new name. She loved showing off her first-born grandson, buggying her little charge around town in and out of the stores. She knew her friends would be there to admire and coo at her little prize. As he got old enough, his Uncle James would also carry him about town on his shoulders to brag and delight the townsfolk.

The following year John lived with his other grandmother, Zona's family: Grandma, Phyla Benson (Goggy), Grandpa Benson (Poppy), and Zona's sisters Dorothy and Nancy. The family lived near the University of Washington. Now Zona was closer to downtown Seattle and the Smith Tower where she worked.

John was still doted on as the first grandchild in the family. However, gone were the days of grandparents thinking it was OK to peel off labels from cans and eat as much butter as he wished. His ration card was the reason they got butter. Life became more structured at the Bensons.

Though life at the Bensons was more structured, the love didn't lessen—only expanded. John's early years were cushioned by the care of not just one, but two sets of devoted grandparents.

JOHN BECOMES A NATIONAL TRAVELER

While Don served overseas, John's childhood unfolded along train tracks and navy ports, tagging along with his mother wherever the war—and his father—called them.

During the time John's father, Don, was in the war, Don would receive a furlough occasionally. Being stationed in the Atlantic, the furloughs always occurred on the East Coast or in the South.

John remembers the stories. His dad's ship might come in to New Orleans or Virginia. His mother would take the train to Chicago and then down to New Orleans or wherever the ship was docked. The next time Don came into port, he would call or telegraph ahead, and Zona would get a train ticket and haul herself and John to that port.

Traveling with a toddler required extra baggage for babies 'needs. It may well have included enough diapers and changes of clothes, bottles, rags, towels, detergent for washing the diapers and clothes by hand on the train, and a few toys. John still has one of his tiny, enameled, metal trucks. When the furlough was over, Zona and John would take the train back to Chicago and on to Seattle. They would bide their time in Washington State until Don called, and once again trek to whichever eastern port the ship had docked.

The first time Zona and John were in Chicago, the smallest change she had was a $5 bill, so she tipped the porter with it. From that time forward, the porter then treated John and his mother as if they were VIPs. All of the porters made sure John was well looked after and were attentive to his mom's needs. They would carry him and all the baggage through the train or to meals in the dining car. John was about one or two years old at the time. The next time his father's ship came in, Zona spotted the same porter, who shouted to his fellow friends, "Take good care of these two."

As an officer, Don and Zona had the pleasure of sightseeing and eating at fancy restaurants. John would tag along. One of the times his mother stayed with his dad for a while in New Orleans while the ship was being repaired. The repair took so long that John learned to talk with a Southern accent.

These early journeys planted in John a comfort with motion, attention to detail, and the calm of being cared for even in unpredictable times—traits that would define his later adventures.

GROWING UP IN SPOKANE

When the war ended, the Earnests began again—this time in Spokane. It was a new chapter and a chance to settle into a more ordinary kind of family life.

When John's dad came back from the war in 1945, they became a united family again. Don resumed his job with the State's Fish and Game, and he was assigned to some of the lakes in the Spokane area, requiring them to move to Spokane. That is where John grew up.

They lived in a duplex in Millwood, east of Spokane, a few blocks from Felts Air Field. John and Zona would watch the little airplanes take off and land. Soon his parents bought the house on Walnut Road. Shortly after they had moved into their new house, Don was off to work south of Spokane for a few days of fish management, the first of many jobs that required days out of town. He came home overnight, then was assigned to go to the north to manage more lakes.

While he was away, Zona was in a car accident with their only car. By the time his dad called home to see how things were going, Zona had to tell him, "Don, I wrecked our car. But the dog is safe. And, oh yes, I just found out I am pregnant!" John was about four years old.

Dad's jobs were always out in the field, that is, managing many of the lakes surrounding Spokane, keeping them well stocked with trout for the fish enthusiasts. He might be required to spend 3 to 5 days out clearing the lakes of junk fish and restocking with trout.

In the fall, Zona was in the later term of her pregnancy and required bed rest while Dad was away. John spent several days feeding and taking care of his mother. Since he knew how to make peanut butter sandwiches and not much else, the pair subsisted on those sandwiches until his father came home. Polly, his sister, was born December 19, 1948.

In those quiet, fish-stocked lakes and peanut butter dinners, the roots of John's independence and creativity were quietly taking hold.

EARLY MODEL BOAT PROJECTS

John's fascination with hydroplanes began with a small wooden kit and a big imagination. What started as a simple hobby would become a lifelong passion.

Back in the '50s, model hydroplanes came out with a kit for a solid balsa wood model. John remembers getting one when he was about 12 years old. It was called *Slo-mo-shun* IV. There were templates to cut out for the shapes, and the shapes were traced onto the balsa. Shapes cut from the wood became the boat parts. The completed boat was powered by a small airplane motor. He was maybe in 9th grade, junior high. Don, Dad, would take his son and neighbor, Terry Jorgens, with him when he was planting fish. They would spend the week north of Spokane at Twin Lakes. Don had a big box filled with live fingerlings from the planting truck and would boat out in the lake and tip the corner of the box to let the little fishes out in different places in the lake.

John and Terry would start Slo- mo and let it loose. Then they used Dad's rowboat with its small motor to go get it.

The next boat, Miss Thriftway, was all balsa-framed and covered with sheets of balsa. John built other boats using the same Miss Thriftway kit for the pattern. Those were the years when the city of Spokane funded the real Miss Spokane hydroplane. He never saw that real hydroplane. He just had models of Maverick, Miss Thriftway, because the kits were designed so several different hydros could be made from a single pattern. The Hydroplane and Raceboat Museum in Kent, Washington, currently sells kits similar to the ones John built.

Then kit manufacturers offered The Thriftway Too model that had a much bigger motor. Terry and John took it to the lake with his dad. They went way out in the lake and started the little hydroplane. When they launched the boat, it went flying in an arc. It could have boomeranged and hit their rowboat or themselves. Instead, it hit the dock. Important lesson learned… safety first. In the middle of high school, he designed a hydro of his own. He named it Tiger, but never did get it finished.

Each boat built brought John closer to the thrill of speed and precision—laying the groundwork for his next chapter: racing.

GO FAST AND TURN LEFT

Radio controls for model hydroplanes had just come out. The boat would only go left, so if you wanted to go right, you had to go left three times. John had seen pictures of boats that ran on tethers, too. The boats raced around and around in the water tied to the tether, and the racers' boats were timed to identify the winner. "Go Fast and Turn Left" became a popular saying during this time. And model hydroplane races began.

There are even t-shirts sold at the Hydroplane Museum that have a boy on a bicycle, turning left, with a model hydro tethered and streaming behind. John was never able to get that kind of boat. It was the end of his high school years. Instead, he sold all his boat hobby to an interested kid down the street and went on to college.

Though he eventually sold his collection to make way for college, John had already caught the current. His love for hydroplanes wasn't over. It was just getting started.

CHAPTER TWO
COLLEGE YEARS AND MARRIAGE

"GET YOUR ASS BEHIND YOU, SPORT"

As high school drew to a close, John's focus shifted. He aimed to graduate with grades good enough to get into college. Though smart, he lacked interest in some subjects, which often left him teetering on the edge of passing. Playing baseball during his junior year on the junior varsity team helped him stay engaged. By senior year, he transitioned to managing the high school baseball teams—a role that gave him purpose, raised his GPA, and ultimately helped secure his spot in college.

With steady encouragement from his parents, Central Washington State College (now Central Washington University) in Ellensburg seemed like the right next step. John graduated high school in the spring of 1962. Before leaving, he sold his balsa wood hydroplane models and equipment to a friend down the road, closing a chapter of boyhood hobbies. With his balsa wood models sold and his high school days behind him, John packed his memories and ambition into a single suitcase. That fall, he hitched a ride from Spokane to Ellensburg, heading to Central Washington State College—ready to carve out his own path.

Campus life was new, but John found his footing quickly. Assigned to North Hall, a brand-new dorm in the heart of campus, he wasted no time exploring. A casual stroll to the field house soon led to a life-changing introduction. There, he met Art Ellis, an upperclassman playing football and the son of one of John's father's coworkers. Art suggested John look into managing the college baseball team and introduced him to Coach Jim Nylander. That casual introduction would go on to define much of his college experience.

John served as the team's manager for all four years. The position didn't just ground him in his new surroundings—it opened the door to friendships and opportunities that would shape his life. Among the players was Don Goetschius, the team's shortstop. John and Don worked together for two years before John met Don's sister, Dianne—the woman he would later ask to marry him.

In the fall of 1962, John graduated from high school and had been accepted at Central Washington State College (now Central Washington University) in Ellensburg, Washington. He hitched a ride from someone in Spokane who was going there, too. So began his college years.

His first three years, he was on campus at North Hall and was assigned a room to himself. It was a new dorm at what is currently about the middle of the campus. It was great. Unnoticed, he brought one of the overstuffed chairs from the lounge and used it in his room for studying. He could tip it on its side and hide it in the spare closet. No one suspected one of the chairs had somehow disappeared.

He was manager of the college baseball team under coach Jim Nylander. Halfway through spring quarter, there was an away game in Spokane with the baseball team. When he came back, he entered his darkened dorm room expecting to get a good night's rest before the next day's classes. A smoky cloud hit his face as he opened the door. Someone was in his room! Puffing on a pipe, Harry Collier said, "I'm your new roommate and you're in trouble. They found the dorm chair in my closet and had to take the closet door off to get it out." It was the beginning of a true friendship that would later help him discover model hydroplane racing. They roomed together for the next two years and became fast friends. Harry would refer to him as Johnnie Jocko since he managed the baseball team throughout his college years. Much later, when John won the "Rookie of the Year" trophy his first year of hydroplane racing, Harry began referring to John as Rookie. Harry's nickname became MV since he was from Maple Valley, Washington. Nicknames are still important in the hydroplane circuit to this day.

John stayed at North Hall until his junior year when he moved off campus to live in an apartment. It was one of a small cluster of cabins behind the hamburger place called U-Totem. The cabin/apartment was a two-room affair: a stove, refrigerator, sink, and kitchen area at one end of the room, and a booth that doubled for table, chairs, and study desk at the other end. The only entrance was a door between the two areas. One bedroom was only large enough for him and his roommate, and a tiny bathroom was big enough to accommodate a toilet, sink, and small shower.

Harry had run out of rent money and so asked if he could pull in a small trailer beside the rental. Harry lived in the 20-foot trailer behind that cabin his junior year at Central Washington State College. He used the cabin refrigerator for his perishables and their bathroom facilities, too. He hooked up the trailer to the apartment power and lived there a whole year. At the beginning of the quarter, after paying his tuition and counting his remaining funds, Harry decided to buy a whole chicken and a box of rice with his last few dollars. Figuring it would last a long time, maybe a couple of weeks, he cooked the chicken in a big pot and added the rice—the whole box of rice! Pretty soon he was adding more water as the rice expanded and then "sitting on the lid," as he described it. He ate from that pot for about a week, then accused John and his roommate of eating out the chicken. It was an interesting year for all parties.

It was the year John met Dianne. She was sitting in front of him in Washington State History class, the requisite for future teachers. John noticed her because she was fumbling, trying to reassemble a mechanical pencil. As he offered to help, he introduced himself. He found out she was the sister of Don Goetschius, the third baseman on the baseball team that John managed. He had known Don from his two years with the team. Shy was John's middle name back then, so he asked Don if Dianne might say yes if he asked her out. Don's declared, "Why don't you just ask her."

A bunch of guys at the dorm had all decided to get dates and go for a grand time. They thought up a fun group activity and each made a pact to invite a girl. Push came to shove, and several excuses were made. No one had the courage to ask or had been lucky enough to get a girl to say yes except John. They all had excuses why they couldn't get dates.

After a few days of pondering how to ask Dianne out, and before he knew the others had had no success in getting dates, he got up the courage and asked if she would like to go ice skating in Yakima. She said yes! The plan was great, except all the other guys didn't follow through.

It was a bit intimidating picking up Don's sister for a date. Their dad was Dr. Donald Goetschius, a professor of education at the college. John hesitated before he rang her doorbell at the appointed time. Would Dr. Goetschius answer? To his surprise and relief, her brother Don answered. When the bunch picked up Dianne, she was the only girl piling into the car with all those guys. She wondered, at first, what kind of date this would be. It turned out to be lots of fun.

Ice skating in Yakima could have been a disaster. John didn't know that roller skating and ice skating require a whole different set of technical skills. Dianne helped John up off the ice at least 25 times. She had grown up in Iowa and had skated since she was very young. It didn't matter. They had a great time. Afterward, all those guys were scratching their heads, wondering why John had such a grand time—he couldn't even skate.

All John and Dianne's dates from then on were just as much fun. By December, John was hooked. During Christmas break, he even called her from Spokane and invited her to come visit his family. Dianne took the bus to Spokane on Christmas Day and met his family with a happy assault of barking dogs to greet her arrival. Within hours of her arrival, John's mother had taken her aside and said, "You are just the girl for my John!" Dianne wasn't sure what to think about that. By winter's end, John was no longer just a baseball manager or a student trying to stay afloat—he was someone in love. The quarters passed quickly, each weekend stitched together by laughter, dances, and study dates with Dianne.

As summer 1966 approached, life opened into new possibilities for both of them. While Dianne flew to Hawaii for summer classes, John took a quieter route—working near Portland and wondering what the next chapter would hold. The following summer, 1966, Dianne and her good friend Barbara Wade took off for eight weeks of summer school at the University of Hawaii. Dianne and Barbara had adventures going to Hawaiian History class and Hawaiian Hula class, touring, playing at the beach, and double dating. It was the Vietnam era. Lots of very homesick military guys were using Hawaii for respite from the war. With each date, John became more and more appealing. Meanwhile, John had a job at the fish hatchery working near Portland that same time. He spent his weekends exploring Portland.

At the end of the summer, when John picked Dianne up from SEATAC airport in Seattle with Harry, he was not sure what to expect. Had she found a new boyfriend? Did she still like him? Dianne and Barbara stepped off the plane. Dianne says she had the best tan she ever had and was eager to see John. She was smiling and holding out a lei. John stood open-mouthed and flat-footed, mute. Harry finally shoved John forward, mumbling, "I think she wants to give you something." Within two weeks, John proposed, and Dianne said yes! They spent the year engaged, finishing their last year at Central.

GRADUATION AND MARRIAGE

June 10, the day before, had been graduation ceremonies—an important day in the Goetschius family. Both Dianne and her brother Don graduated from Central Washington State College with teaching degrees, the day before the wedding. The whole Goetschius family and friends attended, with a party after. At the end of summer school, John would also finish, taking his last class with his father-in-law-to-be.

Saturday, June 11, on his wedding day, John was coaching his Little League team—the last and very important game of the season. His team was playing against the nationally known, famous Central basketball coach, Dean Nickelson, and his Little Leaguers. Harry was John's assistant coach and best man. Pending wedding or not, the game had to go on.

The teams had some talent and were a creative bunch of kids but were new to the game. During one game, Harry, the assistant coach, huddled the kids and said, "Help the pitcher. Talk it up out there!" "What are we supposed to say?" the kids asked. "Just say anything, make a lot of noise." Out to the field they went, armed with their new weapon. From the dugout, Harry finally made out what the kids were saying. Throughout that inning, the fans in the bleachers heard loud and clear, "Anything! Anything! Anything!" and lots of noise. The game tied and went into extra innings. It was an exciting last game of the season.

The game finished, John and his best man, Harry, dashed over to the local Methodist church in Ellensburg. Both finally showed up late, but in time for the wedding. Dianne was happy, with a bit of nervous anticipation. The photographer was a wreck. The groom and best man were late! John was John.

Everyone was finally assembled and in their places—girls just outside the sanctuary at the back of the church, guys at the front just behind a door. Dianne had chosen one of the three pieces the organist had offered for music before the ceremony was to begin. The music began. She played the first choice Dianne had selected. The girls waited for the guys to come out. The guys waited for the maid of honor, John's sister, Polly, to begin, The organist played on and on! She began the first piece again. Brother Don came bounding up the stairs to ask what was wrong. The girls said they were waiting for the guys to begin. Quick thinking on Don's part started the ceremony. He simply picked up Polly and set her down in the sanctuary. There were a few glitches, but Zona, John's mom, said, "This is the most fun wedding I have ever attended."

After the pomp and circumstance, the reception in the downstairs fellowship hall became a jolly affair. Greeting well-wishers at her parents' home after, the couple quietly slipped out the back door and walked the block to Barbara Wade's parents' home, just a block away. Their car was hidden in the garage. They were off for a 10-day honeymoon, touring Oregon and losing their marriage certificate somewhere along the way.

They didn't know about the extra apartment key his former roommate had made before the wedding. The apartment was "rearranged" and a bit messed up when they returned to begin summer school. With a wedding behind them and summer school ahead, John and Dianne stepped into married life surrounded by the same humor and friendships that had shaped their college years. The honeymoon was over, but the adventure had only just begun.

After summer school in Ellensburg, John, taking a final class from his new father-in-law, was ready for his teaching position. The newlyweds moved to Portland, Oregon, to begin their teaching careers. John would complete 30 years as a middle school teacher in Portland Public Schools, beginning with wood shop and industrial arts like his grandfather had done in Seattle Public Schools and finishing his career teaching English and Social Studies.

Dianne taught for two years in Portland and four years in Battle Ground, Washington, where they had moved. She paused her teaching when she became pregnant, then finished her teaching career—one year substitute teaching and 32 more years teaching private piano to many students. John continued in the Portland Public School System and finished his career there.

SUMMER SCHOOL

By the end of their first year of teaching, they knew they would need further education. They did want to travel. Summer school in Colorado reminded Dianne very much of the summers spent in Laramie, Wyoming, when she was a child. Her dad went to school there for four summers, resigning from the Plymouth, Iowa, School District. The last whole year, the family moved, and Don finished at the University of Wyoming, earning his doctorate.

The Earnests had also had enough rain and cloudy days on the West Coast to want to dry out.

The first three summers were spent attending the University of Northern Colorado at Greeley. Dianne aimed for her master's degree. Shop was being phased out in many districts. By the second year of teaching, John realized he needed to diversify his teaching skills. During the three summers in Greeley, Colorado, he changed his aim from shop to classroom teaching, receiving the fifth-year certification for middle school.

Student teaching was one requirement. Although he had already taught for two years and his supervisor had received her certification but never taught in a classroom, John was as much a mentor to his supervisor as he was her student teacher. After three years of summer school, they each had accomplished their aims and had wonderful adventures in Colorado, too.

For two years, the couple tried city life, renting the main floor of a repurposed farmhouse on 20th and Belmont in southeast Portland. The city had grown up around the place.

After the third summer spent in Greeley, the couple decided to move "across the river," where Dianne was hired by the Battle Ground, Washington, School District to teach third grade. With only the Volvo for transportation, they moved into an apartment within walking distance of Dianne's school. Too late, the couple realized that the school districts were too poor to hire a third-year shop teacher. Dianne taught for four more years, then paused teaching when she became pregnant.

EARNEST ACRES BEGINNINGS

After six years of teaching, the Earnests purchased nine acres outside Battle Ground for $1,000 an acre and moved a 14x65-foot Marlette, a brand new mobile home, onto the property. Dianne decided to buy the land by withdrawing her accumulated retirement. In the fall of 1973, their new address was on Dover Road, just outside of Battle Ground. Their daughter, Katherine, was born the following January fourteenth. Family life settled in.

Having lived in furnished apartments until now, they needed to furnish their new home. John's Uncle Si gifted the young parents his old, oversized, 1939 sofa and matching chair. Uncle Si had worked at a furniture store and bought it brand new about 1940. Since Emma and Si had no children, the furniture was still in good condition. Dianne's parents gave them an old dining room table and chairs for the dining room. Since John was still a shop teacher, he built a headboard, coffee table, and matching end tables at Atkinson and Grout Schools to complete furnishing the mobile home with essential furniture.

He used the living room to begin building his first boat, the *Slo-mo-shun* IV. The glass that topped the coffee table became the workshop. He would sit on the couch, draw the patterns on 1/16" plywood. With no jigsaw, he used a wood-burning set to cut out the patterns—not ideal, but creative.

As the boat building continued, the mobile home seemed a bit small. With the house set on a slope and a sliding glass door in a good location off the living room, they decided to add a new, bigger living room with a walk-out basement workshop below. A place for tools and having a space to really work on projects was a great asset for the whole family. The only problem was the addition. Semi-attached to the mobile home, the addition had a waterfall between the two structures. The first time it rained, there was a waterfall between the buildings. Although they opened the sliding doors and used the new room, there was always a leak.

WHY DID THE CHICKEN CROSS THE ROAD?

There are steady characters in our lives, people you might recognize in your own life. Throughout the rest of the book, you will come upon them. Do they resemble anyone you know?

TALES FROM THE WORKSHOP

John always had a workshop, much like his grandfather Robert—the teacher, woodcarver, and furniture builder. John's father had set up a workbench in the basement of their Spokane home on Walnut Road for as long as John could remember. Directly across from the bottom of the stairs, it was just outside John's bedroom door. Nails and hooks on the wall behind the bench gave tools a place to be, although they were likely to be found on the bench or wherever they were last used. His dad's job often kept him away from home for extended days, leaving John to help with home maintenance and tinker on his own.

Although the first few years of John's marriage—spent in a few apartments and moves—meant a time to establish a career, John did not miss having a workshop. Since he taught shop at first, he had access to all the tools and space to work, and he was able to use the space during off hours. The unfinished 20x20-foot addition was built with a small covered deck on the east side of the living room. A fireplace, using red brick from the old Fort Vancouver High School, and a staircase to the basement workshop on the west side of the room, created a wonderful new space upstairs and down. The first year, their 14-foot fir tree for Christmas, cut from neighbor Jim Carner's woods, was a magnificent contrast against the plywood floor and pallet railing around the stairs. It was, however, way bigger than their measly accumulation of 50 ornaments and three strings of lights. Oh, the ambitions of young married couples! With a young dog and a new baby, only a third of the tree was ever decorated. A few years later, when the trailer was hauled away and the rest of the home was built, the stairway was removed.

Meanwhile, the workshop below was taking shape. First was the wooden bench across the south wall, replete with shelves and plywood, cupboard doors. It remains today almost the same as when it was first built, except for the scratches, gashes, and general paint and glue that tell silent stories of projects that graced the bench throughout the years.

Now the electric sander, jigsaw, and vise have become permanent fixtures. The wall above the bench is much like the one in Spokane when he was growing up. Behind the door to the original five outside stairs is a good assortment of handsaws for any wood project. Posters of hydros from the past fill the spaces in between. The east "Wall of Fame" has a vast assortment of pictures of past friends and events. Hanging on the north wall are his favorite model hydroplanes that have been retired from racing.

The west wall has an elevated plywood work table, bandsaw at one end, where nowadays most of the building action takes place. The CD player at the back of the table belts out all his favorite singers—Johnny Cash, Elvis, the Big Bopper, and Buddy Holly—during work sessions.

During the early 1970s, in John's early years of teaching at Ockley Green Middle School, the science room was being repurposed. He brought home an old set of cupboards that just fit inside the space where the living room stairway had been. Back-to-back with the new elevated workbench, it created new storage in the workshop. He also retrieved a door with a grid of frosted glass panes on the upper half, salvaged from the old school, giving the step-down workshop entrance a bit of mystery and intrigue into the fantasy land of the workshop. On walls and tabletops everywhere are boat parts, molds for building, models from racing in years past, as well as hydros that are currently in the racing circuit. The room is a creative, bewildering display of fifty years of accumulated fond memories.

JOHN HOWELL'S VISIT

"Hi, John! Sure! Come over this Saturday. What's on your mind that we can do?"

John Howell lived in Troutdale, Oregon. RCU boaters dubbed him "Carpdale," chuckling. He had good knowledge about building lighter-weight model hydros and enjoyed sharing. They would bounce ideas off each other, and John had a warm basement instead of his own cold garage.

His running conversation, laced with profanities, created a colorful, steady rhythm and comfortable atmosphere as the two discussed the pros and cons of building. Howell was a self-taught expert. His attitude about the boating hobby was the thing that Dianne's husband appreciated, too. It was pals enjoying a favorite pastime together and the stories created during the racing season that endured.

"By Monday, nobody remembers who won," John Howell would always say. "They remember the stories." John Howell would then launch into a story or two about the last races.

Dianne always liked to come down and greet the guys as they came through, perhaps offering them a cup of coffee or lunch if the work session ran through the lunch hour. Otherwise, she left the "boys" alone to make boats.

The east wall is full of past memories. "Who's that guitar player on your wall?" John asked once while he was in the workshop.

"That's Les Ruggles when he sang with a band and was promoting a song he composed. I have that song on a cassette." Then John would play Les's pop tunes on his old cassette player so Howell could hear them. Les was more than an accomplished expert in model hydros.

Looking at another photo, his friend asked, "Where did Dianne get to sit in the replica of the real Hawaii Kai, at Kent in the Raceboat Museum?"

"Yup," was John's reply.

Then Howell spied a barge-like model, long and wide—Miss Wayne.

"Are you really going to try to run that Miss Wayne with two engines like the big boat?"

"It's a good challenge," John responded. He spent a year trying to synchronize the two engines, get them to run at the same time—or at all. Now, in 2024, his old-time buddy, Ron Daum, is building the Miss Wayne and will try his hand at building a seventh-scale electric Miss Wayne to run with two engines.

More than once, Dianne would come home and ask what project he was working on. She could smell it instantly, and it had a dangerous, strong odor that filled the house if it came in from the barn before the fumes had dissipated sufficiently. John used old-time K&B epoxy paint that had to be mixed together. It created quite an odor and permeated everything. When the car barn was built, projects could be left to "cure" away from the house.

TROPHY, I SHOULD HAVE STAYED AT HOME

Safety was always part of John's approach to any project, and he was good at following the rules to be safe. However, he was up at Marysville once, packing up all the equipment and boat to head home. Howell glanced over, then came over to his card table.

"Hey, you're bleeding!" he said in alarm.

John still has no idea how he sliced between two of his fingers toward the end of the race. With a bandage wrapped around his hand, John drove home with John Howell in the passenger seat all the four-plus hours. Dianne was not at home.

"I can take myself to emergency. You head on home. You still have another hour of driving," John volunteered. Howell headed home. John took himself to emergency. He claims it took him longer to get stitched up than it did to drive from Marysville to the emergency room. If one searches through the mass of trophies lining the wall above the freezer, there is a trophy that reads: I Should Have Stayed at Home—trophy for that year.

CREATIVE IDEAS FOR THE MODEL HYDRO HOBBY CAN BE DIFFICULT

There is an old bathtub used as a watering trough for the cows during the summer season. John uses it to dissolve the wax that is used to release the fiberglass from the boat molds. John also checks for leaks by filling the raw hulls with water, making sure there are no pinhole leaks. It is fine if the cows who drink from the tub are not around.

One time, he was using his makeshift paint booth inside the barn since it was raining outside. He kept noticing dust-like problems with the paint. The light caught a fine cloud of dust being kicked up. He could not understand why it was a particularly bad day for painting.

John recalls, "I was painting my *Oh Boy! Oberto*. I had put clear on the boat and said to myself, 'Just perfect!' I went into the car barn next door to get the solvents to clean the spray gun. As I turned back to the old barn, I remember seeing a whole dust screen coming out of the barn door. The chickens were having a dust bath right beside the boat. Some debris got on the boat, of course, but not enough to need repainting."

Makeshift paint booths are tricky. "If there is not a gnat or dust particle on the paint job, it isn't my paint job."

CHAPTER THREE
HYDROPLANE RACING

To understand how John Earnest became hooked on model hydroplanes, it helps to step back into the roots of the sport itself. The pages that follow trace the thrilling rise of hydroplane racing—where it all started, how it grew, and the moment John first felt its pull. John has embraced the sport and built model boats that range from the beginnings, with *Slo-mo-shun* hydros, the first true hydroplanes and the ones that made Seattle and the West Coast a fierce competitor.

BRIEF HISTORY OF HYDROPLANE RACING

The first Gold Cups took place in 1904 on the Hudson River, the Lawrence River, and Manhasset Bay. At the first race, three boats were entered. C.C. Riotte's Standard putted home at the amazing speed of 23.6 mph. The Gold Cup Race was won by a boat named the Vingtet-*Un II.*

In 1915 Miss Detroit entered the competition. Their driver got seasick, and the mechanic had to finish the race.

Gar Wood revolutionized the sport in Detroit, making it a boat-racing town. He began adapting World War I aircraft engines and made famous his long line of Miss Detroits and Miss Americas. In the 1930s, Horace E. Dodge became a competitor during the Depression years, spending $5,000,000 promoting the Gold Cup. This was the beginning of yearly races. He won that race in 1932 with Delphine IV and in 1936 with Impish. George Reis's El Lagarto won three years in a row during that time.

Excerpts from the article, "The Story of the Gold Cup" by Bob Karolevitz Information taken from 52nd Running GOLD CUP Official Regatta Magazine, August 4 through 8, 1959

ANCIENT HISTORY TO SEATTLE WATER FOLLIES

Because Green Lake is significant to John's love of the sport, here is a short history of the lake. Green Lake is one of four lakes carved out by the Vashon Glacier approximately 50,000 years ago.

In 1869, Erhart Seifried, a German immigrant and the first white settler in the Seattle area, homesteaded 132 acres on the northeast shoreline of what is now known as Green Lake. He became known in the area as Green Lake John.

Speedboat races took place as early as the 1930s on the lake. By 1950, the south end of the lake was developed into an Aqua Theater where sellout crowds enjoyed Aqua Follies and theater, and the first Seattle Seafair was born. Boat racing continued on the lake into the 1980s, when boat speeds increased, as did noise and crowds. Hydroplanes and all boat racing were finally banned.

Ref: Jason King article, "Hidden Hydrology," Oct., 2018.

At that point, hydroplanes moved to Lake Washington. Seattle Water Follies became an all time favorite when *Slo-mo-shun* wins brought the Gold Cup races to Seattle four times out of five years.

Back in the early 1960s, the boats were still made out of wood and used engines from WWII airplanes, both American and British. Allison engines were old U.S. P-51 and other fighter planes. The British had Rolls-Royce engines. However, Packard made the engines in Detroit for the U.K. and they were shipped over during the war. They were made lightweight and had lots of horsepower. It is truly an American sport. After the war, many engines were surplus and were comparatively inexpensive. So, hydroplane owners would buy up the engines for very little money.

GREEN LAKE

That rich history of speed and innovation eventually reached John's backyard—both figuratively and literally—when he first witnessed model hydros at Green Lake in Seattle, setting the stage for what would become a lifelong passion.

In the early 1970s, model hydros were still allowed to race for a few years. What a fitting place for John to see his first radio-controlled model boat race.

In the years after the wedding, Harry (MV) was teaching in the Kent school district. John (Johnny Jocko) and Dianne were teaching in Portland, Oregon, but still had fun hanging out together. Harry invited the two to come from Portland to see the action at Green Lake. Harry had told John about a national model hydroplane race in Seattle. The first time John saw radio-controlled hydroplanes in a race was when he, Harry, and Dianne went to the Nationals in the summer of 1973 held at Green Lake in the heart of Seattle, Washington.

Harry was getting serious about model hydroplane driving, too. He told John there was someone at the race he wanted to meet. He said that the guy draws up boat plans for model hydros and he would be there. They wanted to see what it was all about. When they arrived at Green Lake, Harry asked if anyone knew Roger Newton. Someone pointed, "That big guy over there." Roger's regular job was fighting fires, and his size would reassure anyone needing help during an emergency that he would be the one to do the job. The three met Roger and his wife Marty Newton at the race. Roger was drawing up plans for 1/8 scale hydros. At that time, he had only a few sets of plans completed. One of the plans was for Miss Seattle 1/8 scale Harry was hoping to build. John decided on Roger's plan for the *Slo-mo-shun* IV. Harry bought the eighth scale *Slo-mo-shun* V plans but made the Miss Seattle from those plans. Many of the model plans could be used for more than one kind of hydro. The big boats were many times converted to a boat with a new name. The models were to be exact replicas of the unlimited hydroplanes. Hopes were high for scale models to create a racing circuit duplicating the big unlimited boats.

The day was warm at Green Lake. There were spectators from near and far who had come to see what model hydroplane races were like and to enjoy the park. There was even a group from Japan who brought their boats to race. John began taking photos with his new Nikon camera as soon as the car was parked and he was close enough to get some good shots. Tables filled with model hydros and equipment lined the lake on one side, and spectators milled amongst the tables full of boats and equipment to get a close-up view of the action. When boats were running on the water, there was a rush to the lake's edge to see the action of model hydros racing. The sounds of the engines echoed across the lake, and the aroma of nitro fuel permeated the crowd.

The boats were fashioned after hydroplanes from the past and present, some more accurate replicas than others. John wanted to check out how accurate the models were against the real boats and was taking pictures. As the sound of engines blazing caught his attention, he turned his camera toward the water in hopes of getting a good shot of a hydro in action. A boat was coming toward the beach at full speed, and it was obviously out of control. Looking for the hydro through his camera lens, John didn't realize that the boat was headed right at him. Harry and Dianne were yelling, "Look out! Look out!" About that time, the model hydroplane took a slight angle to the right and slammed—with a distinctive smack of splintering wood against wood—into the pickup boat. The owner of the unfortunate hydroplane, radio transmitter in hand, hurried over to collect the pieces. Racing for that day… done. John, however, was hooked.

That summer day at Green Lake wasn't just entertainment—it was a turning point. Inspired by the craftsmanship, community, and sound of nitro-fueled engines, John made a commitment that would shape the next fifty years of his life.

JOHN MAKES A COMMITMENT MODEL HYDROPLANE BUILDING BEGINS

As Roger Newton proved his seriousness about beginning a model hydroplane club, John became a founding member of the Radio Control Unlimited club (RCU).

November, 1973, Letter From Roger Newton

The following is an early letter from Roger Newton explaining recent happenings in District #8 and the basic rules concerning building the model hydroplanes. The postmark on the letter is November 8, 1973. John had met Roger the previous summer at Green Lake. It was probably a letter to organize the first test/race held at Spanaway, Washington.

RACING RULES

1. Boat must be a replica of an unlimited that has raced in the past or is racing at the present time.

2. Standoff Scale: Detail must include driver, full cowl or fake engine.

3. Scale: 1 1/2 inch = 1 foot 0 inches ±5% length ±10% width

4. Registration: All registered boats will be required to get a radio frequency.

5. Qualification: All registered boats will be required to get a qualifying timing (exact procedure to be determined later)

When the different flights are set up for a race, the fastest boat on each freq. goes into Flight 1, second fastest into Flight 2, etc.

This simple 5-rule beginning has expanded over the years so that now there are about 27 pages of rules.

The following is the list of members who were probably charter members of Radio Control Unlimited model hydroplanes:

Boats that are running or under construction:

- U-60 Miss Thrifty – Bizier R/T
- U-54 Wildroot – Charlie R. Daum
- U-37 Miss Seattle – H. Collier
- U-77 Country Boy – B. Peterson
- U-7 Notre Dame – L. Stoddard
- U-77 Miss Wahoo – P. Hanley
- U-27 *Slo-mo-shun* IV – R. Newton
- U-37 *Slo-mo-shun* V – M. Steere
- U-8 Red Man – T. Maggard
- ? – J. Dunlap
- U- Miss Bardahl – G. Weinstein
- U- Hustler – C. Gray
- U-27 *Slo-mo-shun* IV – R. LaCalli
- U-27 *Slo-mo-shun* IV – J. Earnest

About the same time, Roger sent a second letter advertising his Unlimited Scale Hydro Plans. This second letter, probably a bit later, demonstrates the progression of the club in just a short time. He gave additional details concerning hydroplane requirements:

1. Boat must be modeled after an unlimited from the past or present.

2. Power will be by a class 'C' engine, .46 to .67 cu. in.

3. Boats will be built to the scale of 1 1/2" = 1'0" or +10%.

4. Boats to look as scale as possible—must have driver, fake engine or cowl, etc.

5. No restriction on type of construction.

6. Boats in District #8 are to be registered ($5.00) with the Self-Appointed Scale CZAR of Dist. #8. The purpose of this is to regulate the boats to be built and keep from having duplicates.

Note: he already called himself the Czar.

LACAMAS LAKE
ROSE CITY MODEL YACHT CLUB

Later in the summer of 1973, John met with some boaters he had heard about at LaCamas Lake, which is near Camas, Washington. They had several kinds of radio-controlled boats and were experimenting with different kinds of speed boats. It was his first contact with a group of radio- control boaters in the local area. Many would become part of the Rose City Model Yacht Club in Portland. Playing with their boats that day were probably Dave and Sonia Blackstien, Norm Nordby, and Jesse Sheehan.

John decided to join the Rose City Model Yacht Club. Norm Nordby and others were forming a new race boat club that would be in the Portland area. They would use the NAMBA (North American Model Boat Association) for insurance. They could be part of the RCU racing circuit Roger Newton had begun up in the Seattle area. Soon after meeting the boaters at LaCamas Lake, John joined the club to become treasurer and a stalwart member until its close in 2023. The Portland Rose City Model Yacht Club met at Norm Nordby's Hobbies Unlimited Store on Interstate Avenue in Portland. The club had secured a racing spot called Force Lake for practicing and holding races in the Portland area. By this time, John and club members had model hydroplanes ready for competition.

1972–1974 SLO-MO-SHUN 1/8 SCALE NITRO
Boat Building Begins

Harry Collier, college roommate and best man at John's wedding, helped rekindle John's interest in model hydroplanes. Harry built *Miss Seattle* at the same time that John built the *Slo-mo-shun* IV.

In the fall of 1974, John bought plans from Roger Newton and began the building process for his first 1/8th scale hydro, the *Slo-mo-shun* IV. It was designed to use nitro-methane fuel. He decided to build the *Slo-mo-shun* IV, the 1951 version. His eighth-scale *Slo-mo-shun IV* was a different year than Roger Newton's *Slo-mo*. Monte Steere, another boater new to the hobby, had already secured the *Slo-mo-shun* V. John really liked the old boat that made the hydroplane sport popular.

The eighth-scale model boats were made of wood like the old boats and designed to look exactly like a real 28-foot by 11 1/2-foot hydroplane. Using drawings from the "Czar," Roger Newton, who started the sport, John made a grand rendition ready to run. However, it took 2 1/2 years to complete. His teaching career was a high priority since he was the sole breadwinner and new father at the time. He was also meticulous about details. It was the first 1/8th scale model hydroplane he had ever built from scratch. During these early years, the living room addition with a basement for his workshop was built.

Steps to Building a Model Hydroplane

John has built more than 46 boats in his career. He likes lists and a step-by-step approach. These are basic steps John used to build his first wooden model radio-controlled hydroplane.

Materials: waxed paper, 1/2 or 3/4-inch plywood, and 1/8-inch plywood sheeting, Elmer's glue. Plans for the jig are on the plans for the boat.

1. Jig: 1/2-inch or 3/4-inch plywood, the length of the boat body without sponsons, plus the sheeting which covers the frame and is the exact shape of the boat bottom. Cut cross frames and fit to the frame in order to stabilize and give the correct shape.

2. Wax paper: Cover the jig top and sides with wax paper.

3. Using 1/16-inch thickness plywood, the boat bottom and inside of the sponson are tacked to the bottom and sides of the jig using nails.

4. Right and left lengthwise frames from back to front and on the insides of the sponsons along the jig are cut with hollowed-out areas in the plywood to lighten the weight of the boat.

5. Crosswise frames are cut, hollowed out, fit, and glued between the lengthwise frames. The transom is labeled cross frame number one.

6. A horizontal stringer outlines the shape of the sponsons. Sides and bottom of the sponsons are sanded to fit the final shape.

7. The top of the frames is sanded to fit the deck. The deck is glued in place. Mahogany 1/32-inch plywood is stained and glued to the deck. After decals are in place, paint using a catalyst (2-part paint); clear over all. The special paint doesn't react to the fuel the boat uses.

8 Fiberglass cowlings are fit to the deck. The driver (Big Jim doll, legs cut off, body wired to the seat, head filled with foam for flotation), the seat, steering wheel, dashboard are all handmade from aluminum or fiberglass, with details of decals from the hobby store, hand-sewn life jacket. (Body parts of dolls were often found scattered about.)

Drive line, rudder, propeller, and OPS brand, size .60 cubic inch engine. Radio control and rudder servo are put in a waterproof box.

Dialing in the boat is next and could take a season or two. Figure there will be many runs and lots of experimentation.

NEW ARRIVAL AT EARNEST ACRES

January 14, 1974, Daughter Katherine Marie Earnest is Born in 1974, which was a happy distraction and slowed progress toward finishing his first boat and making it ready for racing. She learned to stand and walk using the model to steady herself.

Each time John got stuck over what step was next, the family would go visit Dianne's parents in Ellensburg. On the way, they would stop in Kent, Washington, to look at Harry's boat for answers. This way, John could continue building and putting the hardware into the boat. Harry, having close access to the experts, was able to teach and build boats, too. His *Miss Seattle* was built and ready to go before John completed his racer.

An extra thing John did to assure his boat would look as close to the real thing was choosing the correct wood stain for the deck. He wanted the *Slo-mo-shun* wood deck to be the same color as the real boat, even stained the right color and using mahogany veneer for the deck. John mixed up stained wood samples and sent them to Harry and Les Ruggles. Les, who lived in the Seattle area, had a business called Mutiny Model Marines and at that time was considered a top boat builder. By comparing John's samples with the real *Slo-mo-shun* hydroplane at the downtown Seattle museum, Harry and Les sent back the best choice.

The lettering had to be cut out by hand from Monokote color sheets that had sticky backing. John traced out the letters on the color sheets before cutting out each letter with an exact-o knife. Each letter had to be placed and lined up correctly. After the letters were in place, he applied a clear coat of paint on the boat with a small spray gun.

Meanwhile, Katherine continued to use the boat for her own amusement as he continued to build it on the living room floor. She ensured the boat was sturdy enough to withstand the grueling upcoming races. Since their home was a single-wide Marlette mobile home, it was also the workshop. By the end of 2 years, a one-room addition was built, replete with a basement. That basement is still his workshop, and the walls are covered with many photos and boats of the favorite old models and memorabilia from all the years in the sport.

A combination of nitro methane, methanol, oxide igniters, and a little bit of oil created the fuel used in the boats. For a while, the hobbyists bought the fuel in Seattle from some fool who was mixing it on his own. He would order 50-gallon drums of nitro and methanol and mix the fuel at his home. It was a good deal for the boaters to buy cheap fuel. That ended when the fire department found out. One can imagine the neighborhood hazard he created. After his home operation was shut down, boaters could also order the fuel where it was professionally sold.

About Christmas 1975, the boat was almost ready to run. John had the boat finished by January of 1976. At Christmas time, just before school was off for winter break, a student brought some very tempting chocolate cupcakes, which John enjoyed. By the end of the break, John came down with hepatitis along with several others who had enjoyed those cupcakes. On Katherine's second birthday, she, Dianne, and Dianne's mother were given shots to prevent hepatitis and, with a recovering daddy, were the only ones at her party. It was a real help and comfort to have a grandma look after Katherine while Mom shuttled back and forth to the hospital in Portland and continued another week when John was released from the hospital.

Hepatitis turned out to be an opportunity for John's hobby. During the last week of his six-week recovery, he went to Kent. That February, he went to see Harry and run the *Slo-mo-shun IV* for the first time. Les Ruggles corrected his sponson angles. Then he and Harry took it out to a lake and ran John's Slo-*mo-shun IV*. When Les quit racing in 1978, he had *Miss Supertest* almost completed, and John bought it. He finished the boat and ran it for part of a year. John couldn't find out why it would trip and turn over at higher speeds. Les was no longer there to troubleshoot problems, so John sold the boat.

Though that particular boat didn't stay in the fleet, the lessons John gained—from craftsmanship to camaraderie—became part of the foundation of a hobby that would span decades, build friendships, and fill his workshop with both trophies and treasured memories.

CHAPTER FOUR
BOAT TESTING

February, 1976, Spanaway, Washington

RCU ran *Slo-mo-shun IV* near Spanaway, Washington, east of Tacoma. It was John's first experience in racing. The RCU (Radio Control Unlimited) club held a test race at nearby Lake Tapps. Here I was in Spanaway, Washington, with my new one-eighth-scale rendition of *Slo-mo-shun IV* for its first run ever! Excitement and nerves were front and center all the way up the I-5 freeway from Battle Ground. "The Czar," Roger Newton, and Les Ruggles—boat designers and builders— and a few others were already at Lake Tapps testing their own boats when I arrived. My excitement for the day climbed another notch. Could I set up my equipment in time to race?

JOHN'S MEMORY OF HIS FIRST TRY AT DRIVING

Was Grandma Ide's card table big enough to hold the boat on its stand, starter, cowling, transmitter, and nitro fuel? Had I remembered everything?

Setting up for a boat race on that ancient card table made the euphoria of racing—after two and a half years of building—feel both scary and real. The maiden run, still with rookie status, was close at hand. We were up on a bank for a height advantage to help us see the boats clearly.

Action on the far side of the pond distracted drivers during testing. Someone was taking potshots at the boats. "What the h#*&#?!" Roger exclaimed. He spotted campers sitting in front of a tent with a rifle, laughing and having fun—target practice for them. Not so good for a model hydroplane. He and Les began walking toward the campers. I followed. The guys were living in a tent and just messing around. After the six-foot-four firefighter with a stern expression—Roger Newton—and Les had a talk with them, they stopped shooting. We could finally continue racing.

Gee, I was nervous just before the race during the drivers' meeting. I barely heard Roger and Les explain what to expect, how to drive, and how to start the boat. Someone helped me start the engine and carried the boat to the water. I held the remote-control radio in my hands—the kind with control sticks, not the wheel-control kind. *Slo-mo-shun* was launched, throttle opened, and ZOOM—up on plane! Hydros generally begin low in the water like regular boats, until speed brings them up and on plane, riding only on the sponsons and propeller. First clockwise turn, down the backstretch, and rounding the right-hand turn. Another lap and my confidence was building. Not so hard, I thought.

Then another boat entered the racecourse, also testing! Oh dear! Stay out of the way! Pay attention to my boat only! Concentrate on MY boat. Listen to the guy coaching me through. A couple more rounds and I brought it in. Success! My boat worked. Testing day was a success.

After the drivers' meeting to explain the rules, John was ready for his first race. The drivers and spotters stood on a small bank above the lake. Fifteen boats were racing that day. The race followed rules similar to those used by full-sized hydroplanes.

John remembers that Harry was his spotter—and somehow, he won the first heat. He felt cocky and very excited. In the next heat, he received three penalties and was called off the course—he had run over three buoys and was DEQed (disqualified) for that heat. In the following heat, he had settled his nerves and was back to racing. *Slo-mo* was ready for the upcoming season.

LOOP THE LOOP

The next race was in Portland, at Force Lake in Portland, Oregon. The new Radio Control Model Yacht Club had procured the site near the Expo Center with permission from the Heron Lakes Golf Club. John had spent time during the offseason using his favorite wood, black walnut, to build the trophy—fashioned after the Rose Cup Boat Regatta Trophy. That trophy is still passed from winner to winner in RCU.

They dubbed the race "The Rose Cup," and it was sanctioned as part of the activities during the Rose Festival, held yearly in mid-June.

It was the first Portland race, and all the members helped get the site ready. After permission was granted, weeds and blackberries had to be cleared, and the launch area prepared. A couple of guys rowed out to remove branches and debris from the pond.

On race day, buoys were carefully placed and aligned to resemble a miniature oval, like those used by big hydros—orange buoys, except for the green start buoy and the one at the middle of the backstretch. Two stone walls that formed arcs into the pond at the right turn gave spectators a safe place to park cars and watch the action. Those walls also served as an unusual obstacle—and secret weapon—against drivers unfamiliar with the course. It might have given Rose City an edge, as it was their practice pond.

John went out testing before the race with other racers. After completing his first lap and straightening out on the backstretch, he brought up the engine speed and—just like the real *Slo-mo-shun* IV on one of its early runs—performed a complete loop-the-loop and kept running to finish his laps. He had built the boat so close to Roger Newton's accurate plans that the model behaved just like the full-sized *Slo-mo*. Wow! Race time ready. John drove *Slo-mo-shun IV* for one year.

Points Setup for Racing

When model hydroplane racing began in the 1970s, only boats made from Roger Newton's plans were available. They were all one-eighth-scale, meaning the boats were one-eighth the size of the real hydroplanes. That meant all boats were in a single category and could race together.

Nowadays, there are several classes of boats based on the year they were raced and the boat's scale. There might be Vintage, Classic, or Modern heats. And there might be tenth-scale, eighth- scale, or seventh-scale heats. John even built a fifth-scale *Gale V*, which he donated to the Hydroplane and Race Boat Museum. That scale only saw a few demonstration races. The boats were too big and expensive to transport and run. Fifth-scale models never really raced.

Points are awarded according to the order of finish. First place earns 400 points, second place 300, third 225, fourth 169, fifth 125, and sixth 69 points. The six boats with the highest scores race in a final heat at the end of the day. There are usually two consolation finals with drivers earning half and quarter points for their efforts.

To qualify for the heat, a boat must be up and running on the water 30 seconds before the starting gun. The boats "mill" before the race. The heat begins with a "running start," and each contestant tries to hit the start line at zero on the clock. Running into buoys or cutting off other boats will disqualify a boat from that heat. Flagrant violations can disqualify a boat or driver from the entire race. Many drivers register more than one boat at a race.

In the early days of racing, back in the 1970s, there was only a half-page of rules—about five in total. As the hobby grew, so did the number of rules. Now there are 27 pages of commandments!

John always wanted to be sure he had fellow boaters to race against. Monte Steere, who built the *Slo-mo-shun V*, had once ridden in the real *Slo-mo-shun IV* as a kid. It was a special boat for him. His father had been invited to ride in the big boat but died suddenly before he could. The owners offered Monte the ride instead. John generously offered to lend *Slo-mo-shun IV* to Monte, who drove the boat for a couple of years. John was always generous with his time and talent.

PIT TALK

There is always plenty of "Pit Talk." Throughout this book, there will be pauses for important pit talk information.

How to Outwit Your Opponent

WHY DID THE CHICKEN CROSS THE ROAD

HC: The chicken already crossed the road while you weren't looking.

Harry Collier: Before the first race begins, as you pass by your opponent's table, casually mention that you won't finish any heats today. When your opponent doesn't finish the heat, pass by his table and say, "That's one."

After the second heat, when your opponent's boat tips over, pass by and say, "That's two." By the third heat, just pass by and say, "That's three." Ron Erickson, a top racer, never finished a race that day.

MARCH, 1976 – FIRST RACE AT GREEN LAKE

It was a cold, wet, early March race at Green Lake in Washington State. The weatherman had given a dreary, soggy forecast as the Earnest family left Battle Ground, two hundred miles to the south. The Seattle area was all of that, plus a cold wind off the lake. John figured right for the cold. His hands were so cold he had trouble running the stick controls for speed and turning. The Safeway bread sack covering the Futaba radio transmitter just barely kept his hands dry enough to guide the model hydro. The whole line of drivers and spotters shivered through each round of racing. The combination of occasional gusts and punishing rain proved daunting. He never did warm up all day. The tables and equipment were icy to the touch. Transmitters were encased in plastic bread wrappers in an attempt to keep them from getting wet but needed toweling dry by the end of the first heat.

Coffee in the thermoses was cold by the second heat.

Les Ruggles, his spotter and coach, was urging him to get closer to the buoys. John was practicing while being careful to avoid hitting any of the other boats on the choppy water. Les became more and more agitated and frustrated as he told John to drive inside new, conservative driver Marty Newton's *Hawaii Kai* on the backstretch. As the two raced their boats, John was still not sure of his driving skills. He kept going outside her wide, oval course, almost into the shoreline and weeds. As Ruggles' commands crescendoed, "Go inside Marty!" John kept driving the boat way outside on the edge of the course. John brought his boat to shore, Les stomped off, his patience utterly exhausted.

Marty and John became racing partners for many years, staying outside and being careful not to hit any boats. They raced at Green Lake several more times until Seattle shut down all forms of boat racing on the lake.

Meanwhile, Dianne remembers that race too. It was early spring, with a bitter wind from the north sweeping across Green Lake. When they first arrived, Roger Newton's wife, Marty, invited Katherine and Dianne to share her camper, which was parked across the street from the race site.

Dianne divided her time between Roger and Marty Newton's camper, trying to entertain and keep their 2½-year-old daughter,

Katherine, warm—sitting on a folding chair near the lake, with Katherine on her lap to keep them both warm as they watched the first race of the season.

So began a boat racing career that would span five decades.

SPRING, 1976 – TWIN LAKES, MARYSVILLE
Time Trials
Quality Building and Attention to Detail Pay Off

In the spring of 1976, John found out there were to be official time trials at Twin Lakes in Marysville, Washington. He packed his gear into the 1969 gray, four-door Volvo sedan and headed up I-5 to Twin Lakes. Several of the guys were already there and had set up the straight- line course. A stopwatch sufficed for checking each boat as it tried out the course.

John tried three times to see how fast his boat could go. The first time, *Slo-mo-shun IV* was recorded at about 43 miles per hour. The second time, he got *Slo-mo* up to 45 mph. The third time was consistent but no better. Les Ruggles, who had adjusted John's sponsons earlier in the season, had been watching. "Let me give it a try," he said. He was curious to see what the model hydro could do. He pushed the speed to a bit over 45 mph. "It's as fast as most of the other boats," said Les with satisfaction.

John entered enough races and earned more points than any other first-year boater. At the end of the season, he received the Rookie of the Year trophy. His attention to detail and willingness to ask questions and take advice had paid off.

SUMMER, 1977 – RENO, NEVADA

Slo-mo-shun IV Attending First Nationals

It was an exciting first for John and Dianne in 1977, being part of the model hydro scene. They drove down to Reno, Nevada, with the racing gear and hydroplane after dropping Katherine off in Ellensburg, Washington. Grandpa and Grandma Goetschius were always so generous with their time, and Katherine thrived with both doting grandparents. She, like her father, was the first grandchild on both sides of the family.

Off they went to Reno, Nevada—a very dry place. On the first morning, in spite of drinking lots of water, Dianne became dehydrated and had to be taken from the race site back to the hotel to jump in the pool, cool down, and rehydrate.

As the day heated up, planes were landing at the airport but couldn't take off—there wasn't enough moisture in the air. Reno's high altitude combined with its arid climate kept the boats from running very well, too. Depleted oxygen and dry air prevented any of the boats from performing at their best. Still, they did their best and enjoyed the meet. It was a great experience to race hydros on a national scale. By the end of the first racing season, John had accrued enough points amongst his first year boaters to receive the Rookie of the Year trophy, the beginning of many trophies he would earn in years to come.

VANPORT HISTORY
MODEL HYDROPLANE CONNECTION

During WWII, Vanport, on the Oregon side of the Columbia River, became an important part of the war effort. It was a hub for manufacturing parts. The city remained until the Columbia River floods came through and obliterated it. What remains today is now called the Expo. It's a building formerly used to house detainees—Japanese families—a sad reminder of America's reaction to its own citizens during the Japanese aggression.

The Vanport floods of 1948 wiped out the city, which had been established during the war. Years later, the area became what is now known as Delta Park, a place with soccer fields, a former horse race track, the present Portland International Raceway (PIR), and a stockyard—behind which was a settling pond.

Though the stockyard had long disappeared, the settling pond remained and was repurposed, eventually named Force Lake. It sat at the edge of the new Blue Heron golf course. Boaters used it until the golf course became popular and golfers began to complain that the model hydros were too noisy. In the early days, the lake was the practice site for the Rose City Model Yacht Club.

Several races were held there, including the Rose Festival Hydroplane Race. John made the trophy for the Rose Cup Race, which is still passed from winner to winner today.

UNIQUE INTRODUCTION
John Howell

WHY DID THE CHICKEN CROSS THE ROAD?

JH: I'll be happy to have a running commentary of the chicken crossing the road. Just tell me… or not.

Boaters often met at Force Lake to practice. Force Lake was part of the old Vanport area before the 1948 flood that wiped out the community. When they tried to pound stakes into the ground for the canopies, sometimes they hit the cement of the old foundations.

The drainage pond remained after the cattle yards disappeared and is located near the Expo Center, just off the Heron Lakes Golf Course. There, model boaters had the opportunity to see if their methanol-fueled hydros would run.

It was also where John met John Howell. Howell joined the club around 1980. He eventually built a lighter-weight version of the *Slo-mo-shun* for John Earnest. At that time, John made boats that were too heavy.

John Howell came on the Rose City Model Yacht Club scene during a practice event, where he had his boat on a card table near John's. It was a boat testing day with card tables lined up, drivers fixing boats, and testing their driving skills. There was the usual debris—boat parts, various wrenches, rags, and a gallon of fuel—on John Howell's table. A boater walked by, recognizable by a lit cigarette in his mouth most of the time. After he passed the table, Howell grabbed a rag and began dancing around, holding the rag that was quickly disappearing. The cigarette had caught the rag on fire. Because methanol burns invisibly, no one could see the flame, but it was on fire. You could only see the heat waves.

At first, John and Dianne just watched, thinking maybe this new boater had gone off the deep end—or maybe it was a good-luck ceremonial dance before launching the boat. It was the beginning of a long friendship with John Earnest, built around the hobby of model hydroplane racing.

John Howell's favorite times were at Earnest Acres in the basement workshop making model hydros, stopping in the morning at McDonald's for an Egg McMuffin on race day, or going to dinner at the Chicken Shack after races. There was always a recounting of events and tales of memorable races. Because John had spent more time with John Earnest than with any other boater—racing, building, and traveling—Howell declared that John had more influence on him than anyone else in the club. The races created bonding and many fun tall tales. John always asked Howell for advice, even when it wasn't necessary.

THE WALL, A SECRET WEAPON

Early in Rose City Model Yacht Club racing, Force Lake was their place to gather and practice. They had set up a Detroit River–style racecourse with the big turn at the west (golf course) end, and a narrower corner on the right-hand turn, where the stone parapets on the lake shore were located. They could visit the pond at their leisure to practice during the week. This gave them an advantage since they knew exactly how much room they had before hitting the stone walls.

Guest racers had only a few practice runs on race day.

Those walls gave the Rose City Model Yacht Club a definite edge during at-home races. John just kept collecting points.

John and Dianne at a Rose City Yacht Club race 1980's.

Picture of john and dianne

John said he hit the stone wall once and dropped the engine out of the bottom of the boat. His comment: it didn't hurt the boat any. Only John, who knew how to fix boats, would say something like that.

At that time, the Portland police also had horses to help patrol downtown. In Delta Park, a few acres were set aside to house the horses when they were off duty.

Rain, Nor Ice, Nor Volcanoes Can Keep Hydro Enthusiasts From Their Hobby

WHY DID THE CHICKEN CROSS THE ROAD?

RD: I need an outline of how the chicken is going to cross the road. There needs to be research before it crosses the road and evidence that it knows the road.

This event must be sanctioned. While Ron Daum was still living in the Vancouver area on Blueberry Hill, the Rose City guys decided to go testing. "Hey, come to Force Lake and practice," Gary Duback had called to tell him. Ron remembers it was a beautiful, clear Sunday—May 18, 1980.

At about 7:30 a.m., he heard a large boom. The fighter jets must be practicing today, Ron thought. The Air Force often flew to PDX from Fort Lewis on weekends, using the airport for training.

Ron loaded up his Pinto and drove to Force Lake. "We happily ran our boats all morning. About noon, Norm Nordby's wife, Sue, and my wife, Phyllis, showed up at the pond. The girls had been watching the televised account of Mt. St. Helens erupting in Vancouver's backyard since about 8:30 that morning. They asked, 'What do you think about Mt. St. Helens?'"

The boaters were so engrossed in their practice runs, they hadn't even noticed the black plume of smoke rising 50,000 feet from the top of Mt. St. Helens. They looked up and made a few remarks, then—as hobbyists do—went right back to playing with their boats.

Daddy Knows!!

When Portland police still used horses to patrol downtown, a few acres were set aside to house them when off duty.

In the summer of 1981, Phyllis was pregnant and came to Force Lake with their 18-month-old daughter, Erin, to watch Ron race. They had passed the horses on the way to the lake. When they arrived, Erin marched right up to her daddy, Ron, with an intense scowl on her face and announced, "Cows moo!" Smiling and happy to see her, Ron agreed that cows did indeed moo—unaware of the ongoing argument she'd had with her mother.

Suddenly, a triumphant look crossed Erin's face as she turned to her mother, as if to say, "I told you so!"

Phyllis explained that they had passed by the police horse corral a few minutes earlier. When Erin announced, "Cows moo," Phyllis had kindly explained that those were horses, and horses "neigh." After some back and forth—with Erin scowling and insisting, "Cows moo!"—she came to Daddy. He *knew*.

ROSE CITY MODEL YACHT CLUB

Dallas Cook, who always had comments and stories that kept the races lively, raced in the 1980s.

By the time Dallas Cook became secretary in 1987, he was writing colorful missives about the club. John had been a member since about 1980.

Here is the list of members in the winter of 1987:

1. Dallas Cook – 63,547

2. John Earnest – 57,750

3. Gary Duback – 42,554

4. David Blacken – 26,836

5. John Howell – 23,436

6. Norm Nordby – 20,048

7. Clay Smith – 18,590

8. Larry Knudsen – 17,621

9. Bob Christianson – 3,267

10. Jeff Christianson – 3,181

11. Rich Yeider – 3,003

12. Skip Churchill – 2,010

13. John Montgomery – 1,852

14. Kevin Hardy – 450

15. Jack Yeider – 300

Norm and Susie Nordby offered their home for meetings. Norm owned the "Hobbies Unlimited" hobby store on Interstate near the Swan Island exit.

Dallas had a ready wit and loved renaming people, places, and things, which gave the club notes an interesting and humorous twist—and made the newsletter a fun read. He named the newsletter *Rudd E. Duck* in honor of the resident duck population, whose pond owners threatened club annihilation if a boat even ruffled a single duck feather. Dallas also referred to Force Lake as "the puddle," where they tested and raced their "toy" boats.

He even thoughtfully named the newest "toy" boats in the spring newsletter. The following list is a tribute to his creativity:

- Norm Nordby – '85 Square (Squire) Shop

- Dave Blacksten – Ricky Ricardo Spec.

- Dallas Cook – Another Oh No!

- John Earnest – Miss Spud (Budweiser)

- John Howell – Ms Tingles (Pringles)

- Jack Yeider – Daglo Red Spec

- Clay Smith – Anything Ole Bardahl ever sponsored

In the spring 1988 edition of the newsletter, he reminded members of the story about how the Nordbys' dog/mascot became the leader. Dallas wrote, "Grand Potentate – Henry (the Cocker Spaniel), as you will remember, we asked for nominations (for commodore)... after a long silence, a short woof from the top of the stairs and BINGO we've got a new leader."

The following is a list of boaters John remembers racing against during those years: Harry Collier, Les Ruggles, Roger Newton, and Ron Daum.

Brian Buass was a national record holder for speed and helped John learn how to make a proper mold for building hydroplanes. Later, he borrowed two of John's boats to make those speed records using the *Oh Boy! Oberto* and *Miss Supertest*.

Dallas Cook, who always had comments and stories that kept the races lively, raced in the 1980s.

Ron Daum is one of the founding members and has raced with John since before 1976. He helped make the original half-page of rules. He is still racing.

WORKSHOP TALES THE CUP
It's a Wonderful Life

The Cup had a life of its own.

Passersby noticed it gleaming in the sunlight as they came to admire the model hydros in the pits. The cup, a typical white, porcelain coffee cup—straight-sided and flared at the lip—had a warning that made it stand out: *To my guests: Warning I Make Lousy Coffee.* Its sleek exterior added a subtle watch-out to Grandma Ide's ancient, wobbly, shellacked card table John used at the races. The Cup proudly ensconced one corner of the table.

Most competitors develop certain habits as they learn their sport. The habits develop into rituals that help them get into the "groove," the rhythm of the sport. Since John spent years managing baseball, he was well aware of the baseball rituals and, in fact, developed rituals of his own that helped him as he raced.

Beginning of a saga: It began with arriving at race sites early, the cold from the night before lingering. Coffee is warming and generally gives a shot of liquid alertness. Thus, the habits added to pre-race rituals.

One particular ritual went something like this. Although tables looked cluttered and messy, there was a certain organization on John's card table to make racing most efficient. He also had an order in which he readied the boat: check to be sure there was sufficient fuel for the engine, be sure all correct connections were made, start the engine, turn on the radio transmitter, check to see if it was connecting to the boat receiver, etc. He also found that a swig of coffee from The Cup just as his spotter was taking the boat to the water became an important part of getting in the "groove."

Dallas Cook, who often was in close proximity to John's table, liked coffee too. Because he either forgot to bring his own or especially liked John's coffee, Dallas would occasionally take a gulp of John's coffee when his ran out. Buddy John Howell noticed coffee raids enough times that he gave John a cup that said, "WARNING I Make Lousy Coffee." The gift was appreciated so much, it became a part of the equipment he always took to races. When it broke, gray glue for building the model hydroplanes was used to put The Cup back together. The problem was that John would potentially run out of coffee before all the races were completed.

"The Cup" realized its importance as Dallas, undeterred, continued to enjoy John's coffee, but finally said John's coffee was worse tasting than his grandfather's.

Before one of John's races was about to begin, Dallas grabbed John's coffee mug, took a swig, said, "The coffee's cold!" and promptly threw it out. John had no more coffee. His interrupted ritual must have taken him out of his groove. That race, he said, was the one when he crashed his boat. The coffee cup remained empty and smug.

The Cup's fans lingered when they realized how important The Cup had become—not just to John or the boats, but to the community at large.

Dallas remembers a time when the tune pipe on his boat was HOT, and he cast about for something to cool it down quickly. John's coffee cup was the closest liquid he saw. Paper towel and several dips in the coffee cooled the tune pipe sufficiently, leaving an oily sheen on the coffee's surface. Oops—John was ready for the next race. Dallas said he raised his hand and was about to say something about the coffee, then decided not to let John lose his groove. He said John did not get sick or pass out from the oil-slicked coffee, so Dallas just decided not to tell him.

The Cup remains today as a beacon of light, reminding the boaters of the wonderful adventures and memories it holds. Long ago, after many mishaps, The Cup began to leak. It had to be replaced. The coffee mug now hangs from the rafters in the shop amongst John's memorabilia.

End of a saga—it truly had a wonderful life.

CHAPTER FIVE
SUMMER CIRCUIT, BROWN BOWL AND MORE

I Didn't Know How To Spell Secretary, Now I Are One

Around 1980, Roger Newton asked John to run for the RCU board—a casual suggestion that launched John into an unexpected role. At the first meeting, early in the year, responsibilities were handed out. When the dust cleared, John was given the job of secretary. Spelling and English were not his forte, but he enjoyed being a part.

As with many other years, discussions raged over boat specs, motors, radio controls, and rules. John invited the board to come down to Earnest Acres for the meeting. Dianne could hear the heated arguments over the phone and was a bit nervous by the time the day arrived. Greeting the guys, Dianne cautioned them to have civil discussions, no pounding on the antique table. And if they needed to fight, the front yard was the appropriate place. Members complied. The meeting went well, and Dianne treated them all to a tasty lunch.

It proved how much the RCU club mattered to these men and how working through differences before the season began made for an exciting, fun hobby.

That meeting at Earnest Acres wasn't just about rules—it showed how camaraderie, shared passion, and a touch of Dianne's diplomacy could turn even heated debates into lasting friendships.

EARLY 1980s BROWN BOWL ERA

Before sleek lakeside venues and polished race days, there was the Brown Bowl—a rugged and memorable chapter in RCU's early days. RCU raced there quite a bit, the first year on the obsolete east side settling pond. By the next summer, they switched to the west side pond since the east side was overgrown with blackberries. Every year thereafter, the spring meant cutting back the prolific blackberries taking over pond edges and the narrow gravel road leading to the pond.

The Brown Bowl was just off I-5 on Orillia Road in the Kent Valley near what is now The Hydroplane and Raceboat Museum. The Brown Bowl was the center of many hydro memories that helped Radio Control Unlimited become an active, cohesive part of model hydroplane racing in the Pacific Northwest.

The Brown Bowl got its name, unfortunately, because originally it was a sewer settling pond. The color of the water in the summer months made its name obvious. It was a regular, frequently used race site in the early years of model hydroplane racing, where fond memories of grueling, hot, cold and rainy, mucky, and funny RCU tales were forged. Years later, when Dianne asked her daughter, Katherine, what she remembered about the races, she promptly replied, "I remember they were LOUD (engines 'noise), smelly (hydro fuel), hot (summer), and dirty (Waghop, Tri-Cities especially)."

Despite the mud, blackberry thorns, and sewage pond, the Brown Bowl became a proving ground—not just for boats, but for bonds that would last a lifetime. Here are just a few stories that cemented friendships, waged hot debates, and formed John Earnest's great love of the sport in those early years.

RACING AT THE BROWN BOWL

Race day had a rhythm, and John Earnest had it down to a science. Today was no different—just him, Howell, the Silver Bullet, and the scent of nitro. John Earnest and John Howell were going up to Kent Valley to race their boats.

John had made his list and checked it many times, as was and still is a wise habit he developed:

1. Batteries were charged up for the day of racing.

2. The two lawn mower batteries in the little waterproof box under the deck, which ran the starting motor, were fully charged.

3. Transmitter and receiver batteries had been charged.

4. A plastic gallon fuel can filled with fuel consisting of 45% nitro, methane, ethanol, and oxide igniters… dragster fuel.

5. Card table (still Meme Ide's old card table).

6. Canopy. The canopy back then was a tarp with four poles and strings and spikes to hold it down.

7. A model hydroplane on its stand.

Box full of tools to fix any malfunction or accident.

Racers had a single hydroplane for the race. All the boats back then were built from Roger Newton's carefully "drawn-to-scale" plans. Roger, dubbed the "Czar" by Jerry Dunlap, got the Radio Control Club up and running with the help of his plans and his encouragement to all boaters.

At first, the motors were started by using a rope like those used to start lawn mowers. Soon, however, a belt and a motorized handheld starter replaced the rope to make starting the boats much more reliable.

To make the day more interesting and a tribute to the big hydros, John and participants usually wore T-shirts and jeans, just like those worn by big boat crews when they were working on the real hydroplanes. Sometimes boaters could get hold of a complete outfit like the one for the Budweiser. John wore cowboy hats. Back at that time, Bill Muncey was a popular unlimited hydroplane driver and was always seen at races wearing a cowboy hat.

The day before the race, all required equipment had to go into the car or the truck. Boat and equipment had to be hauled by wheelbarrow from the basement door up to the driveway to be loaded. Most of it would have to be repacked early in the morning (o'dark o'clock) if a buddy, John Howell, came along.

John used his dad's old 1983 diesel-powered five-speed transmission Isuzu pickup, dubbed the Silver Bullet. It was often the mode of transportation on race days. John's dad had bought the pickup brand new in 1983 for hauling his small hunting and fishing boat. He gave it to John when he no longer needed it. A typical Japanese-built truck, it was meant for people of shorter stature, and the little diesel engine had good mileage. There are still John's dad, Don's, homemade fishing flies on the passenger side visor. A canopy protected the model boats and equipment during many hours to and from race sites.

John Howell drove from Troutdale, Oregon, before sunrise to have an early start for the race. The Kent Valley, where the races were located, is about a 2½-hour drive from Battle Ground up the I-5 corridor, and the aim was to be on site by 8:00 or before to set up equipment closest to the boat launch location. Redistribution of boats and equipment happened mostly in the dark and cold before the two could leave the driveway for the race site. Dianne would see "the boys" off, having made a quick breakfast for John.

Carpdale, as John Howell was fondly dubbed by Tri-Cities' Troy McIntyre, kept John Earnest awake with a running dialogue. With very little insulation from road or engine noise, Howell attached a microphone to the bill of his cap. The device had a microphone which attached to John's hearing aid by means of an electric cord. It worked well enough to keep John alert. If they forgot to detach the device at rest areas, they were both yanked back into the truck's cab—a reminder to detach before exiting. John Howell and John Earnest became a racing team in those years. If they started early enough (5:30 a.m.), they could be at the Brown Bowl in time to set up at their chosen spot.

This particular day all went well at first. Boaters had arrived and set up their equipment. The drivers' meeting was completed, and the first set of racers would be headed down the bank to launch their boats into the murky water. It was primitive racing at its best. Second consolation, first consolation, and the final heat would follow three qualification races. To accommodate the many boaters, some heats had four or more races. Consolation races and the Final would round out the race. The day would end with a short recap of the day's race, handing out trophies to winners, and cleanup.

Hydro racers readied their boats at the end of each race day for the next race by adding oil in the engine to prevent rust. If the boat hadn't flipped or collided with obstacles (other boats, buoys, debris) on the race course, it was ready for the next day of racing.

Every race ended with tired arms, gritty gear, and stories to retell—but for John, it was all worth it. The Brown Bowl was home, and racing was life.

SANICAN FOR THE SUMMER

Some race-day details get left out of the glamour shots. The sanican was not one of them.

RCU rented a sanican for the summer. Also dubbed "the confessional" by boater Gary Jensen, it was picked up at summer's end and otherwise never serviced. The tippy outhouse at the road's edge would give an alarming lurch if the user's weight shifted in the slightest. Already on a slant, the sanican also shifted when entered. It never tipped over but was always unsettling to the user. The sanican was more than ripe by August, adding to the racers' tension—used only when the desperate need overrode the race excitement.

If you didn't emerge rattled and a little nauseous, you hadn't truly raced the Brown Bowl. That outhouse? Just another badge of honor.

MAN OVERBOARD!

Every racer has a moment they never live down. For Howell, it came with a splash—and a stench.

As the water level dropped on the Brown Bowl during the summer, its name became more and more evident. The sun shining through boats' rooster tails turned an opaque, amber, manure color. As boats rounded the course, they churned up a visible line of white foam that often lingered to the next race. Accommodations needed to be made by the drivers because the right- hand turn contained more sludge than water. Occasionally, the briny pond would plug the water pickup tube used for cooling the engines on the boats.

Both Johns were doing pretty well, getting the engines to start, boats to the water, and completing most of the races. However, during one race, John Howell's boat died in the right- hand turn. After Howell rowed out to get the boat, he made a fatal mistake. He decided to step out of the rowboat to pick up his dead-in-the-water hydro. He slid his first leg over the side of the boat and reached for the *Savair's Mist*. Not realizing there was deep mud in that turn, his intention was to walk back to shore, hauling the pickup boat behind him. He took the first step out of the pickup boat. When he reached for his *"Savair's Mist"* hydroplane, the starboard of the rowboat tipped up, catching his foot as his first foot sank into the mud. Dallas Cook colorfully explained Howell did a perfect half-gainer as he lost his balance and crash-landed into the stinky water.

"Stay upwind of the guy from Carpdale for the rest of the race," shouted a boater as Howell came slogging his way to shore. There was a distinctive, putrid stench as he neared. The two Johns had come as a racing team in the little 1983 Isuzu. It was a long drive home, windows wide open to keep both Howell and Earnest from gagging.

That ride home with the windows down wasn't just unforgettable—it became RCU legend. The day Howell went overboard was the day the Brown Bowl earned its name all over again.

THE CZAR WINS, IN TWO PLACES, SAME DAY AT THE BROWN BOWL

September 2, 1984

On September 2, 1984, Roger Newton had two priorities: race heats and a hospital delivery room. Somehow, he managed both.

The Czar, Roger Newton, was in a pickle. Race day at the Brown Bowl and his wife, Marty, was at a nearby hospital in hard labor, about to deliver their first baby. What could he do? The boaters, eager to help, found a solution. They rigged the hydro draws for the heats. Roger would be in race one in the first heat, and then race one of the next heat. Roger could dash over to see how Marty was progressing, giving him a longer time at the hospital. As Marty's labor progressed, so did that race. Roger would finish a heat, then leave for the nearby hospital in Renton to check on Marty. By the end of the day, his wife gave birth to a son AND could add to his season points. Dallas Cook noted, "My wife would have killed me!" Roger's love and devotion for the sport aptly dubbed him the Czar. His wife encouragement and faithful assistance helped keep his Czar status. Behind every great person is someone who assists in every way to make and keep that person looking good. Marty was amazing.

That day, Roger earned more than race points. With Marty by his side and a son in his arms, he sealed his legacy as both the Czar of RCU and a devoted family man.

OVERNIGHTS WITH ROGER AND MARTY NEWTON

Near the Brown Bowl was the home of the Czar, Roger Newton. To encourage participants from a greater distance to race, there was a big barbecue and all boaters were invited. Then Roger Newton invited the boaters to stay overnight at his house. Roger and Marty would serve barbecue the night before the race. Afterward, the racers were invited to "bed down" in the living room, enabling those from far away a free night's lodging. It was these times that boaters could become a more cohesive group. John Howell recalls, "They would bed down in the Newton living room and Marty would have breakfast for everyone in the morning before they headed out for the race day." Several stayed overnight. The others, living in the Seattle area close enough, could come to the party and have a good night's sleep at home for the race the next day.

1977 MISS WAYNE 1/8 SCALE

John's next boat was the *Miss Wayne*. The full-size Miss Wayne had two Allison engines and was long and wide. John even tried driving the boat by putting in two engines. On the real boat, one driver would control one engine and drive, and the other would control the second engine and give it the gas. Just like the real boat, the model had two propellers. Since model hydros were not allowed to run two engines, one was a dummy engine. And just like the real boat, it was big and heavy. It finished every heat in the circuit except one, but always last. One year was enough for that boat. It now decorates the wall of his workshop.

PAINTING JOHN HOWELL'S DETROIT RADIOGRAPHICS

John always liked helping other racers to build, change, or fix their boats. He wanted to have worthy opponents to race and therefore was generous with his skill and time. He was often sought after for boat building advice and help, and is just as generous today with his time and knowledge. In those early days, he often did the final paint jobs for people. Here is one of the many boats he painted. It is so easy to mess things up.

The following incident Dianne remembers well:

John showed me the freshly painted Detroit Radiographics he had just completed for John Howell, with his primitive "paint booth" consisting of the old chicken shed or outdoors, weather permitting.

"Honey, come look what I just finished painting. It looks great!" John said.

The photo he used as a color sample was propped up against the boat. Dianne looked at it admiringly and said, "What a beautiful job! It's neat how you switched the colors and put the white where the yellow is in the picture and the yellow where the white is"

"WHAT?!!!!" John exclaimed.

It is soooo easy to do. Tape off for one color—cover the part not to be painted. Pull the tape and reverse the process to paint the next color. He had to repaint the hull completely.

1962 GALE V 1/5 SCALE

In 1978, John worked on building a 1/5th scale 1958 *Gale V*, the one with the bazooka cowling. He could see that it would never run on the racing circuit. He was having trouble getting decals. He did, however, finish the boat and decided to give it to Roger Newton. It is now at the Unlimited Hydroplane and Raceboat Museum.

COUNTRY BOY 1/8 SCALE NITRO

John built the *Country Boy*. He lent the boat to Gale Whitestein because he could not get satisfactory speed out of it. Gale Whitestein tried, too, the next year and was unsuccessful. Not all boats work out.

Early '80s – The Last Turkey Race in Portland, Oregon

The season was over, but RCU racers had one last tradition to uphold—the infamous Turkey Race.

Model hydroplane boaters will do most anything to keep a planned race going once it starts. For the Rose City Model Yacht Club, the Turkey Race was at the end of the year—November, after the season had already finished and just before Thanksgiving. This race was a Portland fun run at Force Lake.

Dianne remembers:

John had gone on ahead to get the race started. Neighbor Glen Carner and I brought the trophy—a frozen turkey. When we showed up at Force Lake in Portland in the morning, the race had not come close to getting underway. Spectators were pacing the beach and standing in clutches, discussing how to get the race going. The chase boat was out on the lake, using its oars to break ice for a race course, and it looked rather hopeless and kind of comical. Glen and I stayed warm in the car and smiled to ourselves as the rower smacked the ice, breaking it into shards that boats could certainly not navigate. The day remained crisp and cold.

After very little success, a car drove up. The driver popped out and enthusiastically announced that he had just come from the Burnt Bridge Spring Creek area in Vancouver and had seen open water. After a short discussion, drivers packed up and caravanned the half-hour from Force Lake to Burnt Bridge in Vancouver, Washington. New venue, down in a hole, just as cold. Some packed their boats down the 20-foot drop into the abyss that was the "pond". There were probably five to eight boats, and the boat race mostly became a boat testing day for only a few brave ones. Glen and Dianne sat in the car on the far side of the little pond to get a better view. The race was basically in the shade, and the day stayed bone- chilling. Norm Nordy was still the club president. A couple of guys did run their boats, but it was difficult to find a place to launch the boats and more difficult to retrieve them. And the pond was not suitable for racing.

The trophy, a frozen turkey, stayed on someone's car hood and never thawed at all. To keep it safe, Dianne decided to put it in the trunk of her car toward the end of the day. Then, not even thinking any more about the racers who were cleaning up the site, Glen and Dianne went home WITH the turkey. The prize had to be delivered later. It was the last time anyone mentioned racing in November.

Frozen trophy in tow, they called it quits. That final frigid November made the point clear: some traditions are best remembered—not repeated.

1962 GALE V REVISITED IN 1982

Second chances sometimes pay off. In 1982, John gave the *Gale V* another shot.

In 1982, John decided to revisit the 1/8th scale nitro 1962 *Gale V*. He built that one, too. The *Gale V* won Best of Scale in 1985, 1986, 1988, and 1989. That one ran very well. He still has the hydro and races it sometimes. He was in the top five, points-wise, for several years.

This version of the *Gale V* didn't just race—it excelled. With trophies in hand and memories in tow, John kept the legacy alive.

CHAPTER SIX
RACING IN TRI-CITIES

As summer heated up across the Pacific Northwest, the next major stop on the model hydroplane calendar was the Tri-Cities—a region long intertwined with full-scale hydroplane history and model racing tradition.

Columbia Park, Benton County, Washington

Columbia Park is located in Benton County, Washington, along the Columbia River. The public park is comprised of 400 acres, Columbia Park East in Kennewick, and Columbia Park West, 50 acres in Richland, creating a 4.5-mile park. Lewis and Clark explored the river up to Bateman Island, located between Richland and Kennewick. Hydroplane racing began on the river, being called the Atomic Cup at first. Hanford Nuclear Plant, close by, was a logical name. Then the race name changed to the Columbia Cup. Tri-Cities has hosted hydroplane races since 1966, known as the Columbia Cup. That first race was to be remembered in another way, too. During the weekend of racing, two men wading in the river stumbled across a human skull. It was determined to be 4,900 years old! It was eventually dubbed the Kennewick Man. Tri-Cities racing for the big hydros became a tradition, racing the last weekend of July, in Kennewick, at Columbia Park.

In 1976, the first RCU club raced in the park on the same weekend for the first time. They used the little pond, a family fishing pond created inside the park and the first warm water pond in the area. Their race was named the Columbia Cup, the same name given to the big hydroplane races on the river. The RCU race was held during big boat testing on Saturday. The full-sized boats raced on the river on Sunday.

An exciting new attraction was added to the Columbia Cup festivities, which continues to be a special day for hydroplanes and model boaters alike. Convenient for spectators to see the action close up, they can view the races from either side of the river. It is a favorite

West Coast race site. To watch an approximately 30-foot boat that weighs about 7,000 pounds, powered by 3,000 hp engines at 130-plus miles per hour, only feet from where you are standing, is a thrill unique to this race.

"Looks exactly like the one I drove!" exclaimed hydroplane driver, Lee Schoenith, holding John's Gale.

In the 1980s, John and Dianne would pack up for a two-day event. It meant getting the boat ready, nitro fuel and all. Back then, only one boat per person was the norm. Still, the popular race would register 50-plus boats on race day. They would also pack summer clothes for Katherine, plan well in advance, and drop Katherine off at her grandparents, Grandpa Don and Grandma Virginia, in Ellensburg. Katherine had special bonding times, and the parents could participate fully in race events. They would head south to Tri-Cities, Washington. It was always a fun time because the big boats would be racing the very next day on the Columbia River, only a stone's throw away.

On the same day the big boats were testing on the Columbia River, RCU had their racing event at the kids 'fishing pond just a few steps from the big hydro pits. Because model boaters had good-looking replicas of many past hydros and present-day big boats, hydro crews were able to dash over to see the big boats and talk with and exchange racing ideas. The drivers and their crews, still in their uniforms from working at the pits across the way, could watch and marvel at the model hydroplanes in the miniature races behaving the same way their real-sized boats ran on the Columbia River. Big boat spectators still come over and watch the model boat races between testing of the big hydros.

It was and is a thrill to race the model boats one day and watch the real ones racing on the river the next day. At one race, Lee Schoenith came over to look at John's Gale V model boat.

He was amazed that it looked like an exact replica of the big boat he had driven. The July weather was hot and dry, the normal temperature 95–105 degrees. Each model boat camp had its own little canopy for protection from the brutal sun, but it was still hot. Ice down shirt fronts helped keep boaters cool, and stepping into the water to launch boats gave some relief, too. Forty to fifty model hydroplanes and crews would be in attendance, with crowds from the big boat pits wandering over to take in the action. Sometimes there were 200 spectators at a time cheering on the scale boats.

Most participants had just one boat. All types of boats ran together. That is, older, dated round- nose boats and current pickle forks competed together. The designs were from the same basic plans using Roger Newton's many different plans and fashioned into many different replicas of the real hydroplanes. It was the premier race of the season, so attendance was high and still attracts many hobbyists today.

The Tri-Cities became more than a race location. It was a rite of passage each summer, where scale racers brushed shoulders with the legends of the big boats and thrilled crowds with boats a fraction of the size—but equal in spirit.

SANDY SHORE, CROSSED WIRES

Not every race went smoothly, especially on a course where spectators mingled near the waterline and communication could be tricky.

A race site with so many spectators, some used to swimming or fishing in the pond, could become a dangerous affair. Racing with his built Budweiser at Tri-Cities one summer, John was waiting for Howell to tell him when to begin the right-hand turn at the end of the backstretch. Each lap, John turned a bit wider, not hearing Howell's urging to, "come farther into the course! You're too wide!" By the time Earnest did hear, it was too late. He came around even wider on the right-hand turn for the third time and slid Budweiser right up on the sandy beach. Howell said, "What happened?" John's comment: "I don't know." Best-laid plans don't always work. Off at a fast sprint, John went around the pond to pick up his hydroplane as the surprised crowd began to gather around the errant boat to see what happened. Luckily, the caution tape kept the crowd at bay. Unharmed, the boat made the race that day, picking up points and thrilling the crowd.

The crowd loved the unexpected moment, and the story of the beached Budweiser would become part of Tri-Cities racing lore.

LUCKY GIRL, LUCKY BOAT CLUB
Rules Change for More Safety

Safety was still evolving at the Columbia Cup, and one close call served as a wake-up call to all involved.

At Columbia Cup race, the boats were milling and practicing before a race. At that time, during the Columbia Cup, RCU could run their boats with swimmers at one end of the pond away from the boats—or so they reasoned. A girl was out swimming at the far end.

A model boat lost control, and part of the boat, probably the sharp turn fin, grazed her shoulder. She was cut and needed medical attention. Nowadays, if people get near the water or if dogs or ducks are on the racecourse, the race is stopped until the parties at risk have removed themselves. Everyone realized how much worse that injury could have been had it cut her neck. NAMBA would have become involved immediately.

CAUTION TAPE and NO SWIMMING signs began being used at every race to control the spectators. They were welcomed into the pit area only between heats. Signs and caution tape are also used now to keep eager, unsuspecting spectators out of the water and away from the shoreline.

It was a sobering reminder that even miniature boats carried real risks—and that safety would need to grow alongside the sport.

HOWARD PRICE, CANTANKEROUS, COLORFUL, COMMITTED

Among the many characters who made the races memorable, none stood out quite like Howard Price.

Howard Price was a model hydroplane racer known for his colorful language and audacious behavior and his great skill at fashioning tiny metal parts for the model hydros. It is another reason why John received honors for his "Best of Scale" models. During one of the races, Howard Price's boat quit. He grumbled down to the pickup boat.

In those days, people were lax about wearing life jackets. Howard was well known for not following rules anyway. Out he rowed to pick up his "dead in the water" boat. Things were going alright until he reached over the side of the boat to grab and pull his model hydro closer. When the pickup boat tipped a bit too far, over the side he went. He disappeared. After a time, all were watching and becoming a bit concerned.

He came up sputtering and mad. He had left his waders on—no life jacket. He effectively went to the bottom of the muddy pond in a permanent way. In order to resurface, he had to ditch his waders, not an easy feat underwater. If it scared Howard, we will never know. By the time he reached shore, his ranting and raving over losing his favorite sun glasses could be heard all over the pits. His boat returned unharmed. But he lost his boots and glasses. Colorful fellow, Howard Price.

Howard's antics were legendary, and stories like his dive into the muddy pond became as much a part of race folklore as any trophy.

SPECTATORS BEWARE

As the sport advanced and speeds climbed, keeping spectators—and race officials—safe became a greater challenge.

In order for the hydro drivers to see the racecourse better, temporary scaffolding is usually set up near the shore for the drivers and pit persons. Stairs were generally ladders scaling the scaffolding. Sometimes there were six drivers and six spotters cheek to jowl, radio controls in hand, racing the six-lap heats. As the boats had better designs and became more stable, the boats raced at faster speeds.

"Go fast and turn left" was a favorite T-shirt to wear around the pits, an old saying from John's childhood. He and his friends would pretend to be race drivers and race their little model boats. Attached to a string behind their bikes, they sped round and round imitating the races.

The eighth-scale boats, however, went the opposite direction of the big boats. In those days, and still today, some model boat engines run in the opposite direction from the big World War II Allison engines. As Ron Erickson said, "Why fight torque,". The model propellers were fashioned to turn boats the opposite direction of the full-side hydros. The eighth-scale boats ran counterclockwise on the course.

One boat with a particularly aggressive driver was pushing his hydro to its limits before the race. Coming around the left-hand turn, something happened to his radio. He lost control of the boat. There was no steering or speed control and no engine shut-off. As the hydro careened around that last turn, it came toward the shore. Airborne, it grazed a rock and headed straight at the scaffolding and drivers. Under the scaffolding, the scoring table was ideal for watching the race and being part of the action for the contest director. Like referees during a football game, they are sometimes part of the action more than they could realize.

Taking flight, it took a high-flying bounce off the rock on the shoreline, tipped on its side, and hit the steel scaffolding full on. Pieces flew everywhere. The boat disintegrated into a million pieces before everyone's eyes. Had it not hit the rock, it might have hit the people at the scoring table or the stunned crowd that was watching. There was an air-sucking silence after an "Oooooo" from the spectators—a scary, exciting day. It was further evidence that RCU had to keep the spectators safely out of the water and back from the shoreline and that model hydroplanes could be as exciting and dangerous as the big hydros—a graphic incident that helped to create safety measures that are still in use today.

The crash was a jarring reminder that even scale racing required serious precautions. From that day forward, safety wasn't just encouraged—it was enforced.

1988 ROSE CUP
In Portland with the 1962 Gale V

The 1988 season brought heightened stakes and tighter competition, and at the Rose Cup in Portland, John Earnest was aiming high.

Early in the 1988 season at the Rose Cup in Portland, Oregon, John's goal was to gain enough points to be at the top and receive the first-place trophy for the year. The first time out, he nailed the start. That means he was full throttle across the start/finish line just as the starting clock wound down to zero—a great beginning. In his rush to maintain the lead, he moved inside to lane one a bit too soon. His rooster tail hosed down Don Mock's boat, causing it to quit. The CD (contest director) decided it was John changing lanes too soon that had caused the problem. Being disqualified cost him some points. This mistake became important at the end of the season when he was only barely at the top of points earned.

John was out for the points those years and still is. His philosophy is to finish race, boat in one piece, rather than take chances that would result in his boat blowing over. Reckless driving could disqualify him, and jeopardize the odds for the high-points trophy of the year.

At the end of the 1988 season, he was using the 1962 Gale V. He was doing well in the first couple of heats. He was right up there at the very top in season points. At the same time he was running the *Gale*, he was building the 1962 Budweiser. He didn't want to damage the boat he was racing. Caution was his motto for the next race with the *Gale V*.

While the disqualification stung, it fueled a more cautious, points-focused approach that kept John in the hunt through the end of the season.

TWIN LAKES AT MARYSVILLE
Last Race of the Season

As the season drew to a close, one final showdown would decide it all.

The last race of the year was up at Marysville. Rick Campbell, a highly competitive opponent with the *Sutphen Spirit*, and John with the *1962 Gale V* were tied for points. They had both won all their preliminary heats. In this last race, the tie would be broken, and the winner would take home the high-points trophy for the year and all the glory. The tension was like the high string on a violin.

The *Gale V* and the *Sutphen Spirit* came around for the start. Being a bit too cautious, John ran a little wide to save his boat from getting banged up. John Howell was screaming in his ear, "Get lane one! Get lane one!" Howell kept yelling, "Get inside! Get inside!" John stayed a little wide so he wouldn't damage the boat. By then it was too late. Rick Campbell had taken lane one. John pushed *Sutphen Spirit* hard for five laps, but Rick never flinched. He could John catch the *Sutphen* Spirit. Rick won by just a few boat lengths. The race was a nail-biter, but Rick won that last race and high- points trophy for the 1988 year. John had to remind himself that he did come in second against those other 50 or so model hydroplanes. He did, however, win the high-points trophy in RCMYC that year with 11,615 points and for the most points ever scored by an RCMYC member competing in the RCU club.

Though he missed the RCU title by inches, John's season remained one of personal bests— solidifying him as a top contender in the growing model hydro scene.

TOP OF THE SPACE NEEDLE WITH FRAN MUNCEY

The awards banquet at the end of the year was held in Seattle at the Space Needle. It was a night to be fondly remembered. It was so special to eat as the restaurant slowly revolved.

Because of the revolving Space Needle, by the end of the banquet, the party had seen all four directions of downtown Seattle. To Dianne's relief, yes, she could eat the meal and not feel queasy because of the changing scenery.

Fran Muncey spoke about her late husband, Bill Muncey. It was a special honor for John to receive his trophy for second-place points from the wife of the legendary hydroplane driver. Czar Newton and Fran Muncey passed out the trophies. Looking back, it was a very special awards banquet.

1982 *BUDWEISER*, 1/8 SCALE

By the next racing season, John had completed the building of the *Budweiser*. It was ready to run in 1989. Because he had a new 1982 Budweiser almost completed and it was nine nitty- gritty years before he retired, stress from teaching almost 30 years was catching up with him.

The Bud was a beautiful boat. It ran well. He had won Best of Scale with it. However, one day when waxing it up, John noticed it did not have the wood grain on the deck. He was missing the old wood grain look. He got out Harry Collier's plans for the *Gale VII* and once again made a wood grain-looking boat. Larry Knudsen wanted the Bud, so he sold it to Larry.

RACING TIPS
Dallas Cook

In the summer 1989 Red E. Duck newsletter are Dallas Cook's helpful tips to winning a race:

"One thing I have noticed that can help win races, particularly for the new drivers, is dialing in your starts. The first three years I raced in RCU I used the modified 'Shotgun approach. 'With 15 seconds to the gun, I would aim for the middle of the pack and when the field wound-'em up, I'd let go with both barrels and usually hit myself square in the ass. Sound familiar? Needless to say, you do not win many heats by jumping the gun, having the first clear racing lane be number 14, or blowing over by running up some guy's rooster tail. I got lucky and had Butch Melwski pit for me once... Butch's system was a series of timed marks around the course that, if hit correctly, would put you on the line, wide open, at '0. 'You launched your boat at 2:30 seconds to the start and proceeded half throttle to his one-minute checkpoint, the 30-second marker, and so on. It worked then and still works now... In essence, you know where you are going to be rather than hoping to get lucky."

1989 SPOKANE RACE, BE CAREFUL WHAT YOU SAY

At a Spokane race, John Earnest was coaching John Howell. He was half a lap ahead, and John bragged, "You're so far ahead of everyone you can win this race unless someone cuts the course and T-bones you." Don Mock came across, and sure enough, Howell got T-boned.

John had subtle ways of competing similar to the big boat drivers. Don Mock, a highly skilled, competitive racer, liked to unsettle drivers by racing so close to a boat that it was almost bump- and-run racing. John decided to have a talk with him about coming so close to his boat. He went over to Mock's table on race day, talked boats a bit, and asked how much Mock's boat weighed. Mock proudly announced it was 12 pounds and so light it helped to increase the boat's speed. John casually mentioned that his boat weighed 18 pounds, and if Don accidentally hit his boat, The Gale would maybe have skid marks, but Don's boat would most likely splinter or sustain heavy damage at best. Pit talk advice for Mock, echoes of his friend, Harry Collier, at a long-ago race with Ron Erickson.

There were many other race sites during the 1980s. They chose the sites which would fulfill their requirements: small enough to keep from having great waves whipped up by the wind, place to launch, shore cleared for ample visibility of the whole course, not a place where swimmers and shore lovers would be. Especially popular were the few sites with lakes side by side. Force Lake, Portland, Oregon; Elma; Waughop Lake near Tacoma; Marysville Twin Lakes; Rowena on the Oregon side of the Columbia River; Spokane in town; Tri-Cities; Wenatchee; Ellensburg; Rock Island Dam; near Selah, Washington; Celeste Joy were other sites.

BRAD LEWIS, INFORMATION GURU

Brad Lewis grew up with the big boats. His father was a URC official, Director of Marketing and Public Relations, Inspector. Later, he was in charge of the pits. Because of that exposure to many boat race seasons, he was a wealth of information. His dad was in charge of the pits and Brad worked in the pit.

One of Brad's first memories of John was at Force Lake with Kim Hayes, Norm Nordby, Bill Amick, Dallas Cook, and Tom Maxfield. It was a Rose Cup Model Yacht Club event.

It was 1988, and John was still teaching. Brad was impressed by the fact that John was the most conservative driver, didn't want to hurt his boat or anybody else's.

Brad went to Texas in 1998 and was in Houston for 11 years. When he returned to Portland, he and John had much more in common. He was looking at John and sports differently. They now love talking history of hydroplane racing.

THE DAY THE PIGS FLEW
A Story About Brad Lewis by Dallas Cook

Every club has its Cinderella story—and Brad Lewis, with his battered "pig," delivered one of the best.

Another colorful character among the unsung heroes of the Rose City Model Yacht Club was Dallas Cook from Seaside, Oregon. His secretary/editor/newsletter kept members eager to read the next missive, sent out between 1980 and 1987, with his clever quips and comments and newsy letter.

In 1989, Larry Knudsen, a competitive member, had a boat that had had many races under its hull. He decided to sell it. He sold it to Brad Lewis. The boat had been in lots of exciting, thrilling races and had many bumps, bangs, and crashes to prove it. Dallas Cook claimed the bottom of both sponsons were solid Bondo Larry had used to fix the crunches. Dallas likened it to a pig plowing through the water.

It had won races and was a fast boat but had seen its best days. Brad Lewis bought the fixer- upper and started the racing season with the boat. He really had a tough time with it since it was battered and had new problems with each new race. Dallas also noted when it did run, it was capable of any race. He did get it running and one day won a race.

The following is Dallas Cook's play-by-play account. He was calling the race that day and, in his usual grand style, recounted that the boat had won. This excerpt about Brad Lewis's win with Larry Knudsen's cast-off boat is taken from a 1989 RCU newsletter, titled:

"The Day the Pigs Flew"

At 8:04 A.M. any poll would have projected an RCMYC victory in the Gold Cup, or the Bill Muncey Memorial at about 1,000 to 1, and that may have been on the long side of the odds sheet. Too many fast boats, and too many seasoned drivers, and too much event prestige combining to

deal Portland a no-hope scenario… all you had to do was ask anybody. David Jensen won the Gold Cup.

Only moments before, RCU was shaken to the roots by one of the bigger upsets in the last several seasons in RCU. Rookie Brad Lewis, driving the Olympia Beer, overhauled Terry Olding not once, but twice to win the Bill Muncey Memorial final. Taking three laps to pull even with Olding's Exide for the first time, and Brad went for lane one and got a very wet door slammed in his face… Saving a sputtering engine, Brad challenged again on the final lap and out-accelerated the U-75 to the line for his first career victory.

Yes, Virginia, it was truly a day when the pigs nosed into the wind and soared with the chickens.

At the end of the season, when trophies were handed out, Brad Lewis received a trophy for his win. Rose City Model Yacht Club also gave the boater a special trophy for being able to win races with the boat. The trophy was a reworked bowling trophy and had Lewis's name engraved on the stand. The statue adorning the trophy was, of course, a lovely golden pig. John Earnest, meanwhile, was gaining experience and points.

It wasn't just a race win. It was a victory for persistence, camaraderie, and the idea that even the most unlikely boats could take flight.

CHAPTER SEVEN
GETTING RACE READY, ELECTRIC

The electric era brought a new rhythm to racing. Gone were the rope-start motors, gas cans, and nitro fumes. In their place: batteries, silent thrust, and a cleaner setup. The transition wasn't just mechanical—it reshaped the way racers prepared, powered, and protected their boats. These lithium batteries require recharging after each heat and avoiding water as much as possible. Many changes using electric motors for power were made. Transmitters were basically the same. However, now the receiver is incorporated into the circuitry that runs the motor.

Much simpler and cleaner. Now, a small generator is required to recharge hydro batteries in between heats, replacing the need to refuel between heats. Another improvement is that now canopies are pop-up tarps with built-in collapsible legs and trim that directs the runoff downward, all in one for easier setup and more protection from the weather—no separate tarps and poles.

Most races are now held on the west side of Washington State, the wet side of the mountains, making canopies important to keep boaters and their equipment dry, instead of being used to protect from the sun.

At the beginning of the electric era, John Howell built a lighter-weight version of the *Slo-mo-shun* for John Earnest. At that time, John made boats that were too heavy to compete effectively.

BORST PARK CENTRALIA, WASHINGTON
Know What to Do and Who to Ask

As electric racing settled into routine, Borst Park in Centralia emerged as a favored site— convenient, scenic, and central for ERCU racers. It also became the stage for one unforgettable morning that put both planning and patience to the test. Located centrally on the Washington I-5 corridor just off the Centralia exit, it was handy for ERCU boaters, as well as being popular for its many outlet stores. For several years, John chose that park to act as CD (Contest Director), a job shared with members of the club. As CD, he was in charge of seeing that the ERCU (Electric Radio Control Unlimited) club had secured the pond at Borst Park and was responsible for race equipment for the event.

There was an interesting incident that will long be remembered. It turned out well, thanks to a silver tongued model boater with good sense and the Centralia Police Department that Sunday morning. John and Dianne traveled the hour or so up I-5, stopping at Exit 72 for a quick egg/sausage McMuffin at McDonald's. They were well in time to arrive at the park before the boaters. This time, John was the Contest Director. It was, as usual, the first race of the season. The weather forecasters had rightly predicted intermittent clouds and rain and a snowy beginning. It would warm later in the morning but began with rain and a chilly, biting early April wind. Sure enough, rain mixed with snow was pelting them as they turned into the park.

Big trees hid the pond from view as the road meandered amongst them, past the gang bathrooms and baseball fields, around the perimeter of the five-acre park—a one-way asphalt road. There were picnic tables scattered throughout, some with covered shelters typical of Pacific Northwest parks. As John and Dianne followed the little road around counterclockwise, just before it exited to the parking lot, the pond finally came into view.

The pond was deserted except for two fishermen who were down the 14 shallow steps that led into the pond where the model hydro racers could more easily launch their boats. The pair didn't take much notice of the fishermen, except they had all their fishing equipment in tow.

John figured to himself that they would be gone by the time club members arrived and racing activities would begin.

The rain was not quitting, so after surveying the scene for a bit, John and Dianne unloaded their canopy, generator, table, chairs, boats, and equipment that would sustain his boat for the day's activities. By the time their canopy was up, other boaters began to arrive, choosing a site to set up their equipment. By 9:00, the day was in full swing. Boaters were hesitating to launch their boats because the fishermen were still in place and didn't appear to want to vacate.

The ERCU truck hauling a trailer full of equipment for the race soon arrived. Unlike the earliest races when only individuals and their boats showed up, the ERCU trailer contained speakers and microphones that would broadcast each heat and keep boaters informed. It had a computer set up to automatically make the draw for each of the heats to keep things straight and keep the heats moving along. There was also a small outboard electric propeller for the chase boat. The little boat was perched on top of the trailer.

When the chase boat was taken down the steps to be put in the water, the fishermen objected and fished on. John went down and politely told them that the pond had been reserved for a day of boat racing. One of the fellows turned, only slightly acknowledging John, and said in an unfriendly way, "We were here first. Call the cops if you want to." They obviously were ready to argue and stay on. John climbed back up the steps and relayed their message to Nelson Holmberg, the club commodore who had reserved the pond. Nelson talked with the fishermen and repeated the fact the pond was reserved and asked if they could please leave. It was obvious from the raised voices and belligerent stance the fishermen were not leaving. So Nelson went back down and said if they didn't leave on their own, he would have to call the police to help them leave. They both laughed, and one said, "Go ahead. Call the police! We live here." And so, having no other options, that is exactly what he did.

In about 15 minutes, a police car showed up. The policeman first took photos of the fishermen fishing. Then he walked casually down to talk with the fishermen, giving them just enough time to return their catch to the water. Dianne did not want to see what would happen next and went for a long walk around the park.

When she returned, the fishermen were gone. Curious, she asked John what happened. John relayed the tale. The first officer had asked to see their licenses and was told that their licenses were back in the car. When they went to the car to get the official papers, the fishermen asked to see the officer's supervisor. The officer told them his supervisor was in the second car, which had conveniently just driven up, if they would like to speak to him. After a bit of discussion, the fishermen left.

The officer came to Nelson and John and quietly told them what had transpired. The officer had said to the fishermen, "The license needs to be on you and not in your truck. That's a $75 fine. And your license was not signed. That's another $75 fine. If you had caught a fish, that would have been a felony, and you would have been arrested. This pond is reserved for children and handicapped individuals, plus you were fishing out of season."

The whole thing could have devolved into an ugly shouting match and put an awkward twist to the beginning of the race, but John and Nelson Holmberg wisely had preplanned by contacting the city and police beforehand. Taking the high road by being polite and knowing what to do, the cold, damp day brightened, and the first hydroplane race of the season could begin.

Since it was John's birthday, a cake midway through the races made it even more cheery. John and Dianne used old Safeway slickers for the rain. John got those when he retired from working at Safeway for 10 years after retiring from teaching. It always made a curious statement at race sites. Imagine boaters and their spotters lined up racing—John and Dianne had on bright red slickers with a huge, white-encircled "S" on their backs. The weather improved by day's end. Camaraderie and the boat racing hobby were at their best.

The soggy start faded into memory as laughter and friendly competition took over. With cake for John's birthday and the red Safeway slickers making their usual appearance, the day ended with full hearts and dry decks—proof that preparation, kindness, and a little help from the local police can turn a tense start into a successful opener for the season.

GALE VII BEST OF SHOW MISSING WOOD BOATS

While modern boats had their appeal, John never stopped missing the look and feel of true wood. The *Budweiser* hydroplane was a beautiful boat. It ran well. However, one day when waxing it up, John realized it did not have the wood grain on the deck. He loves the old boats that have real wooden decks, so in 1991 and 1992, he got out Harry Collier's old plans for the *Gale VII* and built another *Gale*. It was a real wood boat with mahogany on the deck. Using fiberglass, he created a beautiful mahogany replica of the deck, imitating the grain and each 8x12 piece of plywood, nails and all. The full-size *Gale VII* was the longest and widest hydroplane ever built at the time. It was 36 ft. long and almost 14 ft. wide. John's 1/8th scale *Gale VII* was a beautiful boat and ran especially well if the water was rough. If it happened to be a smooth water, windless day, he was kind of handicapped. The boat only liked rough water. He ran it two or three years. He began to struggle as he experimented with different motors, propellers, tuned pipes. He tried many ideas but could not find a winning combination. Though he gave up, he still has the boat.

Though he eventually parked the boat, unable to find that elusive winning combination, the *Gale VII* remained one of his favorites—a reminder that sometimes, craftsmanship and character matter more than trophies.

MARK GRAN THANK YOU

Racing brings all kinds of people together—and every now and then, it brings the right ones. Mark Gran, a passionate hobbyist, met John in ERCU. Mark had registered the *Breathless II* but hadn't built it yet. John had just finished building a *Breathless II* for Brad Lewis. Brad had not yet registered the boat. There was a bit of a controversy over who would get the registration to drive the boat — the new member without a boat but registered, or Brad, with the boat but no registration. John was driving a *Gale* boat at the time and came over to meet Mark. John explained that he had just finished building the Breathless for Brad. The controversy began and ended quickly when Mark graciously let Brad have the registration. Mark remembers John being a clean racer and a gentleman. What a nice compliment. Mark is a boater he would like to race with any time.

That brief encounter left a lasting impression. In a sport driven by precision and passion, it was Mark's grace that stood out. John never forgot it—and always welcomed a chance to race alongside him.

1992 TUALATIN RACE
Ahead of His Time

The Tualatin race in 1992 was supposed to be just another sunny day at the pond—but for John, it turned into a test of patience, innovation, and grace under pressure. The five-acre manmade pond, with its waterfall at one end, created a town center for Tualatin. It would be exciting for the Earnest racing team because John was trying some new suggestions given to him by his friend and mentor, Brian Buaas. It seemed as if John had incorporated enough innovative tweaks that other drivers were beginning to notice. Some must have felt threatened that he might have a race advantage because of the new ideas he had incorporated.

Practice before the race consisted of a few warm-up laps by various drivers, area cordoned off with caution tape, speakers set up at each end of the temporary pits. The day promised to be sunny and free of wind, at least for the morning. When drivers 'meeting was called at about 10:00, just before the first heat, rules were set out and the usual speeches made about the idiosyncrasies of the course: tight on the far left-hand corner or you will hit the cement wall, and do NOT hit the ducks. Then focus eventually turned to John's boat setup. It was deemed that John's motor connectors were illegal. Somehow, no one had informed him until then.

Connectors for the batteries to the engine were all of a sudden the culprit. Without proper connectors, he could not be part of the race. He had not brought extra connectors that other boaters were using, nor had he been informed until that moment his were not legal for this race. He could have argued or cried foul and stomped off angrily. But true to his sportsmanship ethics, John Earnest simply smiled, shook hands with the CD, and bowed out of the race. John noted in the family November 1990 Christmas newsletter:

"When all is said and done, the RCU Rulebook is always the most difficult to understand when you are losing the argument."

Ron Daum

Interestingly enough, by the next year many boaters were using the connectors that John was not allowed to use that day. He was just ahead of his time. He left without racing, knowing that soon everyone would be following his new idea.

It was still an exciting day. The Earnest family was to greet Stine Norgaard from Denmark. John, Dianne, and Katherine picked up Stine that afternoon. Their foreign exchange student, through the Youth For Understanding Organization, came back to visit the Earnests and friends she had made during her year-long stay at Earnest Acres. Daughter Katherine followed Stine back to her home to be an exchange student the following year at Stine's home in Denmark and fell in love with Denmark. She and her husband, Joel, and their children have lived in Denmark many years, becoming citizens several years ago.

Though disqualified, John left the race without bitterness—just quiet confidence. The connectors that benched him would soon become standard, proof he wasn't behind the times—he was ahead of them. The day ended not with a trophy, but with a reunion that underscored what racing was really about: community, family, and the shared joy of the journey.

Time Away from Boating

CHAPTER EIGHT
TIME FOR MODEL A ERA

Helping Mom, Zona

John retired from teaching in 1997. At that time, he and Dianne began monthly trips to Spokane to help his mother. His dad had died recently, and increasingly, Zona needed help. This monthly routine went on for about 10 years, leaving little time for following the racing circuit.

Although John was no longer building or racing boats, his workshop remained filled with models. Nothing was sold off. The hydro workshop just became dormant.

A new barn was erected in front of the old barn, thinking they would need it for hay from the field. However, he quit haying and having cows and brought home Dianne's grandmother's 1949 Chevrolet from Ellensburg, Washington. The barn now became a car barn. The 1949 DeLuxe Chevrolet Tudor Coupe was a nice car but not as old a car as John really wanted.

John was interested in cars—vintage cars—like the vintage hydroplanes he used for racing. Eventually, the car was passed to sister Connie and brother-in-law Craig, who eventually passed the car to to son-in-law, and race car driver, Erin Strong, and daughter Melissa.

As life slowed in one area, improvements around the home opened up new possibilities.

LOOK MA, THEY HAVE A FREEWAY

Meanwhile, back at the Earnest Acres, Paul Ritola, a neighbor who had just retired from road construction work, was asked to put a bit of cement between Earnests 'daylight basement and the barns. In winter months, the area was always a muddy mess. What began as a path from the daylight basement to the barn expanded into a cement expanse about 50x60 feet! When their friend, Karsten Walther, saw it for the first time, he exclaimed to his wife, Annie, "Come look, Ma, they have a freeway!" With a gravel road to the wide cement slab, there was enough room for three or four vehicles and space to turn around. It made the basement door easy access to Dianne's piano studio and the boat workshop, as well as a clean path to the barns. Work smarter, not harder was the rule. The antique car hobby came into full swing. Dianne could make a sunny basement room for her piano studio. Parents could drive down to drop off charges for lessons, keeping the upper driveway clear for other activities. Many years with two pianos and two keyboards, plus John's workshop, kept the basement humming with activity.

While the driveway took shape outside, John's interest in classic cars began to take shape within.

FINDING THE HEIDELHAUS
The First Model A

In 1991, shortly before John retired from Oakley Green Middle School, he had a faculty get- together at the Alabi Restaurant on Interstate Avenue, just down from Oakley Green, in Portland, Oregon, where he was teaching. He happened to notice some Model A's across the street and looked at them just for fun. On the way home from visiting their daughter, Katherine, going to school at Linfield College, John again made a stop across the street from the Alabi, where Tom Godish lived. After meeting him and talking Model A's, Tom Godish said he knew where there was a Model A for sale and gave us the address in Hillsboro.

After looking it over, John bought it. Long-time friend Bill Shaw helped bring it home. The sellers said they had the car running. When he got home and inspected the car, although it did run, it had no cotter pins securing any of the bolts. It was a 1930 Fordor sedan body, minus interior.

When they wiped off the driver's side door, they discovered the words "The Traditional Heidelhaus." They christened it "The Traditional Heidelhaus" and figured it must have been used to advertise and deliver their product. The interior was all gone—a bit of a disappointment. Tom said to be sure to look up Don and Ruby Knudsen.

John called them. They said they would be at the April swap meet at the Portland Expo Center. After the meet, Don came to look at the car and said it could be restored, but it would take an awful lot of work.

That first project sparked not just a hobby—but a tradition of naming each car with purpose and pride.

HOW MODEL A'S GOT THEIR NAMES
The Tale Begins

There must be an explanation of how these antique A's get their names.

Bill Wilkerson's Fordor is named "Henry's Lady and the Tramp." Bill acquired his black town sedan Model A and often rode around with his collie dog until he met Karel. From that time forward, the dog stayed home, and the Lady (Karel) and the Tramp (Bill) enjoyed the ride. And so she was named.

Dick Bay's "April" was named because he began restoring the winning mauve coupe in April of 1993 and finished the A in April of 1997.

The" Traditional Heidelhaus" kind of named itself. John Earnest's next car," Brush Prairie Lady," was named because the original owners of the black Fordor were two brothers who lived in Brush Prairie. His next car, a Woodie Wagon, was christened "Zona B." in honor of his mother.

Floyd Hickel's "Old Yeller"—can you guess why he named it that? Yes, the school bus yellow paint on that pickup made it obvious.

The Traditional Heidelhaus

In 1991, he bought a 1930 Tudor (two-door). It was a fixer-upper for sure. The seller said there was lots of wood in the car, but the wood didn't show. John was disappointed. As an industrial arts teacher and the grandson of a woodworking industrial arts teacher, John always liked working with wood, and he wanted the wood to show. However, he took the engine out and had it restored at Alan Sherman's Machine Shop. He put the body overhead in the barn and began working on the chassis.

The Heidelhaus had an intriguing history. However, after a few years, John realized the car would require far more time and patience than he was willing to set aside. Because he wanted a driver sooner than he could reconstruct the '30, he looked for another ready-to-run car. He sold the Heidelhaus almost in the same shape as when he bought it and looked for something more complete.

In 1993, in John's quest to find '30 parts, he and Dianne stopped at Al Hollan's home in Micah, Washington. Al had a 1929 Woody Wagon. He explained he had parts for another one which he was selling. Although the thought was tempting, John kept looking for a car that was in running condition.

John and Dianne joined the Volcano A's Model A club and began attending meetings at the Rosemere Grange near Clark College in Vancouver, Washington.

There was an ad in the Columbian telling about a 1929 Model A for sale. They called the number, and Bill Marshall, retired owner of Bill Marshall Ford of Vancouver, said the car was at his house—would we like to come see it?

We paid $7,250, and we drove it to Don and Ruby Knudsen's home to show it off. Don knew the car because he and Art Pugsley had helped restore it for Bill Marshall. He knew the headliner had been damaged and mice had lived up there. Otherwise, it was in working condition—a much better prospect for driving right away.

Bill Marshall had kept this Model A because it had been purchased for $843.80 at his dealership as a new car in 1929 by brothers who lived in the Brush Prairie area. They had never driven it out of Clark County. The two traded in the 1929 black Fordor for a new 1965 Ford Fairlane. Bill had the original bill of sale of the Model A and a picture shaking hands with the brothers as they stood in front of the two cars. Bill gave them a scrapbook detailing information about the Model A to John and Dianne. They christened the A with the name" Prairie Lady" because it had stayed in Clark County from 1929 until 1995.

With the cars came community—and soon, John and Dianne found themselves part of something bigger.

VOLCANO A'S CLUB
John and Dianne joined Volcano A's in 1995.

The club had already been in existence since 1983. Mark Finn decided to work on forming a club that was on the Washington side of the Columbia River. It is actually an offshoot of the Beaver Model A Chapter in Oregon. They would need 10–12 members and a place to meet—only in Vancouver, Washington. At first, they met at a trailer court and in members 'homes. When the Earnests joined in 1995, the club had established Rosemere Grange in the Rosemere neighborhood, Vancouver, Washington, for regular monthly meetings. Every second Monday, monthly evenings were at the grange hall. It was a simple, rectangular room—a kitchen and bathroom at one end. Old wood floors, long tables, and Frank Springer entertaining the club with his Boogie-Woogie on the resident piano. Club attendance increased until the parking lot became too small for parking their Model A's.

In 1998, the Volcano A's moved to Nazarene Church on Fourth Plain where they held meetings for many years. The club membership had beautiful Model A's that were full of personality.

Meetings discussing the hobby of Model A'ing, making new friendships, driving Model A's with lots of tours, kicking tires in the parking lot, dressing up in old clothes, and having old-fashioned fun ensued. John and Dianne were able to drive Prairie Lady to meetings.

As he had done with the model hydroplane hobby, John liked to participate in an active way. In 1996, he was elected president of the Volcano A club. There developed a bonding in the new club that led to planning and successfully sponsoring a regional event. The club sponsored a Regional Meet in 1997. Planning and discussions for the event had already begun with past presidents, Don and Ruby Knudsen. They decided to name the event, "Model A Heaven in '97." With many pitching in to help, especially from former presidents Don and Ruby and the Beaver Chapter, the regional meet took place at Jantzen Beach, just across the Columbia River in Portland, Oregon.

Part of the week's many activities was a tour. John and Dianne used their Prairie Lady, that had never been out of Clark County, to lead Model A's over the Columbia River and up the Columbia Gorge. Over 100 Model A Fords followed Prairie Lady across the Glenn

Jackson Bridge and east up I-84 to Cascade Locks, where participants parked their cars and boarded the Portland Spirit sternwheeler for a boat ride upriver through the locks, to Bonneville Dam and back. At Cascade Locks, there was a delicious salmon bake for all who participated, with time to enjoy the rest of the day and make their way back to the hotel.

The meet was very successful and reaped a $20,000 bonus that has been used as seed money for club events since. It compared to receiving a top trophy at the end of a boat race season. John loved the challenge the same as when he was boat racing.

Among friends and Model A enthusiasts, new adventures rolled into view.

PRAIRIE LADY, SECOND MODEL A Goes to Calgary, Canada

The longest tour the couple took was the tour to Calgary, Canada. It created stories that have become legends in their own right. Long-range plans were made. There would be several small groups from the Volcano A's club going. John and Dianne packed up their Prairie Lady and began the journey with the Thompsons, Gene and Marlene.

Gene liked to wait until the very last minute and was always barely ready, even for this kind of tour. He had been up all night readying his 1930 shiny, red roadster, with the top down, for the trip and was, therefore, very exhausted. Starting early, the groups met up for breakfast in The Dalles, then each group headed out to reconnect at a hotel in Walla Walla, Washington. John and Dianne were following the Thompsons east on I-84 for about 45 minutes. All of a sudden, Dianne spotted Gene's left rear tire wobbling and then slipping off! It rolled to the center divider at 45 or so miles an hour and jumped the barrier. The first car in the oncoming lanes missed the rolling tire, but next, a big rig hit the tire, spitting it over the bank toward the river. Gene wobbled off to the side of the road just before the Deschutes River bridge, the Prairie Lady just behind it.

Before Dianne could say, "DON'T!" John jumped out of the car and ran across the lanes of I-84, jumped the barrier, ran across the oncoming lanes, and disappeared over the side. The trajectory of the tire and the direction of the flowing Columbia assured there was no way anyone would see that tire until it passed The Dalles or beyond. After about five tense minutes, John was climbing the bank and coming into view, carrying the renegade tire! When he had successfully recrossed I-84 and was back by the cars, he explained that the tire, in fact, was in the river and headed toward Portland, but the wind was blowing so hard that the bobbing tire blew upstream and back to shore! Gene had a spare, but no adequate jack. After a 45-minute wait and lots of ideas, a kindly police officer stopped just in time to help put the finishing touches on securing the spare tire. Earnests and Thompsons limped into Biggs, the closest town.

With the break over and nerves settled, they were on their way again. By this time, Gene Thompson was driving on an empty fuel tank—his own. He was very tired. At some point out of Biggs on the way to Walla Walla, the Earnests noticed Gene's driving was becoming erratic. He was falling asleep! As his car swayed back and forth and John ooga-ed his horn, the roadster slowed, which was fortunate. Within a mile, he veered off to the right side of the road and into a rock wall, tipping the car up on two wheels and spilling Marlene out. Fortunately, the car came back down on all four wheels, spun around, missing Marlene. Marlene was OK, but all four fenders were damaged.

"More awake but unfazed," Gene said, "I'll just call my son in Tri-Cities. He can haul the car to his place." And he did. His son said he would bring his rig and haul him to his ranch.

Gene and Marlene waved the Earnests on to their overnight destination, Walla Walla, knowing their son would soon be to the rescue. After resting in Walla Walla overnight, John and Dianne hooked up with another group and traveled for the rest of the trip through Idaho and on to Calgary.

In Montana, they traversed Glacier National Park. The Road to the Sun through Glacier Park is perfect for a Model A with its narrow, winding roads. Cars can only travel about 25 miles per hour, making the scenes all the more breathtaking. The caravan finished in Calgary, Canada—a three-day trip.

When they arrived, there were Gene and Marlene Thompson, sitting in the hotel lobby! "Oh," said Gene, "We borrowed our son's SUV and came on up. Oh, and since I forgot my wallet and driver's license, I had Marlene drive us over the border." Gene and Marlene did not mind being at the edge of danger. This is not recommended nowadays.

On the way home, John and Dianne hooked up with some new friends, Del and Julianne Williams. Del and Julianne were seasoned Model A enthusiasts, and Del had good knowledge about traveling in a Model A. Following a 1930 Tudor made the trip home equally pleasurable, minus heart-stopping events. The two-car caravan passed through Spokane. The four stopped at John's mother's home in Spokane before continuing on to Vancouver. Del charmed Zona, who presented them all with a good snack and good conversation before they continued toward Vancouver.

The only problem the Earnests had with their Model A on the whole trip was a failing horn in Calgary. Off to the repair tent for a fix-up, and it worked again. A very sound car for a 1,000-mile tour!

ERA CLOTHING COMPETITION

"Whether you think you can or can't, You are probably right." Henry Ford John and Dianne also enjoyed competing in modeling era clothing. They modeled era clothing at several regional banquets, receiving added recognition and points. John loved competing and acquiring points just as he had with hydroplanes.

The couple also modeled the era bathing suits at an afternoon tea held during one of the Regional Meets. Like his boats, he scoured the antique stores for clothing and accessories. His outfit, replete with a wool leisure suit, silk vest, shirt with cufflinks and celluloid collar, underwear, socks with garters, dress leather brown saddle shoes, pocket watch, spectacles, cigarette case, whiskey flask, money, and a bowler. Dianne's brown spectator suit to be worn at sporting events consisted of a straight skirt, beige silk sleeveless top, and matching suit jacket. A cloche, matching gloves and purse, slip, seamed nylons with garters, and brown lace shoes created head turns when the two modeled or came to events in costume.

A President's Tour to Lincoln City on the coast gave John and Dianne a photo opportunity to model their lovely, scratchy, navy blue, woolen, era bathing suits with the Pacific Ocean in the background. Ginny Bay was a grand photographer. Leader Jack Dusenbury had a motto for that tour: "No car left behind!" Jerry Lane led the tour back home, stopping at beaches, lighthouses, Tillamook Cheese Factory, and the Spruce Goose Aviation Museum. And all 18 cars stayed together—no one was left behind.

WOODIE WAGON THIRD MODEL A Edsel Ford, Creator

The name of the man whose idea it was to create a Ford station wagon in 1928 was never written down. It didn't need to be. The fact that Edsel Ford kept the first one for himself and gave the second one to his longtime friend, C.W. Avery, pretty well tells the story. (Henry Ford's son built the Woodie, which his father criticized heavily. Edsel had struck out on his own, an affront to his dad.)

Consulting engineer T. Hardy Hayes actually drew the first scale drawings of the proposed 1929 Ford Station Wagon.

In the fall of 1928, Murray completed the first prototype Model A Station Wagon. The car was destined for Edsel's summer home in Maine. Soon after, the second prototype was built. This one Edsel gave to longtime friend, president and chairman of the board of Murray Corporation of America, C.W. Avery, to keep and road test. Avery's daughter, Annabelle Baxley, 7 years old at the time, remembers it well. Down through the years, her family always referred to it as "the prototype."

"It was a wood-bodied station wagon developed by Murray for Edsel Ford," she says. "Dad drove it to get the bugs out before they went into production, and I remember when we took a trip from Detroit to Colorado, and up Pike's Peak. Later, he sold it to Uncle Bill Cooke, who used it on camping trips."

In January 1929, the first Ford station wagons were officially introduced. It was the beginning of one of the most memorable series of automobiles in American history.

Excerpt from the book, <u>Famous Ford Woodies,</u> by Lorin Sorensen.

2000–2004 RESTORING THE WOODIE WAGON

John asked a good friend who owned a Woodie Wagon if the correct spelling was Woody or Woodie. He said, "It all depends on if you think of the car as a girl or a boy car." When John named his car in honor of his mother Zona, the correct spelling became Woodie.

Model A Woodies are a unique design of Model A. The body is made completely of wood. Only the frame is metal. An innovative design and beautiful maple and birch wood on the outside, using spar varnish to make a shiny, waterproof exterior, was a winning combination to pique John's interest.

Woodies are sometimes known as the first travel campers. Dianne had seen an old photo of a Woodie. The tailgate had been replaced with vertical, hinged doors. On the left-hand door, there was an oval tub hanging from a hook. Inside, on the right, was a Murphy bed propped on its side, leaving a narrow galley. Behind the driver's seat was a sink and faucet. On top of the wagon was a water reservoir that attached to the faucet inside. All the amenities that were needed to make camping a luxurious improvement over tent camping.

In 1994, John and Dianne had met Al Hollan from Mica, Washington, who showed them his Woodie wagons and explained he had parts for another one which he was selling.

In the fall of 1998, John was still thinking about his love of working with wood. His next automobile was from Mica, Washington. He called Al Hollan back to see if the Woodie, plus parts, was still for sale. He wanted to work on a car with the wood showing on the outside.

On May 10, 1999, Art Pugsley and Al Hollan brought "most" of the parts and some beautiful wood already cut and ready for fitting and finishing that would replace the damaged or missing parts. The wood pattern in this Woodie is particularly beautiful, as it is cut from one piece of maple, and the grains match all the way across the front and back doors. The Woodie had been changed into a pickup over the years and then basically abandoned.

Al Hollan had a Cheshire cat grin. John was beyond excitement. Dianne asked, "Did you actually pay money for this trailer load, bucket of bolts?" John could see the vision. Dianne saw a bunch of rusty parts.

Five and one-half years later, she had to eat her words. A stunning 1929 Woodie was resurrected from the rust and rotten wood. There were enough original parts that John decided to try to use all original parts in the restoration process. Since he is a Model A judge, John spent many hours studying the judging standards book in the quest to find original or original-looking parts.

At this time, he also became a member of the Woodie Wagon Special Interest Club and bought newsletters, all the way back to their beginning, for detailed restoration information. With the help of many people, the Woodie slowly came together. It was a fun hobby— different from hydroplanes, which required summer traveling and tension to compete on the racing circuit.

Then, when he discovered the National Meet was coming to Portland in 2004, the hobby of finishing the car became a more urgent project as he tried to have it ready in time for the meet. He began working on the Woodie full-time, logging over 1,700 hours and five and a half years of time spent on the project. The car barn was a bustle of activity, with the Prairie Lady beside, watching it take shape.

NAMING THE WOODIE — THE ZONA B.

John began restoring the Woodie Wagon while his mom was still living in Spokane. She had a play-by-play account each month, as John came to take care of her home maintenance, bills, and health care. Naming the car Zona B. (Benson), after his mother, was a natural choice. She watched it take shape for four years.

With the Woodie nearing completion, a new challenge rolled into view, the National Meet. It was to be held at Jantzen Beach, just across the river from Vancouver, Washington, twenty minutes from Earnest Acres.

MODEL A NATIONAL MEET

Getting the 1929 Woodie wagon ready for judging by summer became more than an exciting work in progress, it became an obsession. The club helped so much. If it weren't for the Volcano A club and friends, the Woodie would not have made it to the meet. John and Dianne met new Model A enthusiasts, as well as reacquainting themselves with friends from past meets. They discovered that neither a gas tank full of mouse nest, nor difficulty finding a trailer to transport the fledgling auto, would deter the Woodie from its lofty goal: competing for an Award of Excellence at the 2004 National Meet.

This was reminiscent of those old Best of Show medals John enjoyed getting from his model hydroplanes he produced down in his basement workshop.

It was the night before the meet. John began putting gas in the tank for a test run. As the tank filled, a mouse nest floated to the top—dry grass, sticks, and all floating on top of the gas. What a shock. John came in, despondent and exhausted, to relay the news to Dianne.

The nest had been in the bottom of the tank. Oh, no! At that point, he was tired and discouraged and decided he could not get the car ready for the competition at Nationals the next day. To take their minds off the huge disappointment, Dianne took John out for a quiet dinner.

At about 9:30 that night, his friend Del Williams called and asked if he was ready for tomorrow's judging. John explained about finding the nest in the gas tank and that they couldn't take it to judging. Del shot back, "Get out there and begin running gas through the tank! Use a sieve to extract the debris. Just keep doing that until there is no more nest!"

Spurred on, John and Dianne went out to the car barn about 10:30 p.m. and began the process. After what was hours, the gas began to come out of the tank without any debris. In the morning, he called on his brother-in-law, Don, and his wife, and Dianne's friend, Kaye, to come shine it up for the meet. They did a marvelous job. The Woodie shone. The engine didn't sound very strong, but John got it going after some fits and starts.

Greg Weast, who owned a music store in Hood River, had brought his music trailer to the meet. A Model A driver and hydroplane racing enthusiast, he and John had known each other for many years. He called and volunteered to bring his music trailer to haul Zona B. to the meet.

When he arrived, they measured to be sure it would fit. The trailer was not tall enough to fit the tall car. No more meet.

When all was almost lost, a kind, generous man from Canada called to say he had a truck with a flatbed and tie-downs. Before he arrived, John had managed to get the car from the barn to the driveway.

More fits and starts, but the Woodie finally started up. John drove it up the ramp and onto the flatbed. The guys who came were tying down the car. John was on the flatbed in the car that was still running, anxiously saying, "No, this won't work!"

"Put John in the truck between you two guys! Don't let him out until you are at the meet!" Dianne whispered to the guys. They did as instructed and put John in the truck between them and let him out at the Nationals at Jantzen Beach. He was there and had no more excuses.

When Dianne arrived, the car was in the showroom with all the other cars to be judged and looking stunning. Several people had been so impressed that they lent him additional original parts for the Woodie to help him receive more judging points.

John was standing beside the Woodie in costume, complete with plus fours, matching long red socks and vest, white shirt, bow tie, cap, and vintage-era lace saddle shoes. John looked nervous but handsome standing beside the car. Dianne made a quick stop at the ladies restroom to change into her green apple, oriental-patterned beach pajamas outfit, sandals, and oversized sun hat.

After false starts with lingering mouse nest-in-gas-tank problems, a broken carburetor, and clogged filters, the Woodie made it to the 2004 National Model A meet in Portland! It sputtered around the required mile to prove it would run. It received 416 points and the Award of Excellence! His wood shop grandfather, Grandpe Robert, would have been so proud.

This hobby gained a wealth of friends—willing to help, generous with their knowledge, and enthusiastic at the possibility of getting the Woodie to the National Meet. It was a great learning process, and now John knows Woodie Model A's from bumper to bumper.

Even if you don't have a car judged, learning how a Model A runs can be enjoyable and give one a confidence boost to drive the old car.

The Zona B. has become a fair-weather car. That is, the canvas side curtains with their tiny windows have never been added. The car has been in several Fourth of July parades in Ridgefield, at the Battle Ground Harvest Days parade, and the Hot Summer Nights Gala. It also gives rides to friends, for wedding events, and families on sunny days. It has only been on a few local tours.

One tour that Dianne fondly remembers was at Christmastime, seeing the lights of Battle Ground, Meadow Glade, and Dollars Corner. After the best pizza at Rocky's in Battle Ground, John drove the 1929 Woodie wagon—minus side curtains—the whole way. John did the driving while invited guest Dianne's brother, Don, and Dianne sang Christmas carols and got an unobstructed, chilly view of all the Yuletide lights in the neighborhoods close to their church on 199th Street. Maybe Don and Dianne made up the following little Jingle Bells song just for the fun of it.

The Zona B. didn't just shine on the showroom floor—it carried years of love, labor, and legacy with every polished curve.

JINGLE BELLS, WOODIE STYLE

Dashing down the road,

In an open Woodie A,

Over the hills we go,

Laughing all the way.

Warm, warm clothes we're wearing,

Songs and stories sharing,

Lights a-gleaming,

carols singing,

In an open Woodie A!

Chorus:

Oogah horns, Oogah horns, Oogah, all the way!

Oh, what fun it is to ride In a 4-cylinder Model A.

Oogah horns, Oogah horns, Oogah, all the way!

Oh, what fun it is to ride In a 4-cylinder Model A (with side curtains down),

Even if a change in the weather.

CHAPTER NINE
BACK TO THE MODEL HYDROPLANE HOBBY

SLO-MO-SHUN IV 1/10 SCALE, ELECTRIC

In August 2006, John's mother moved to Battle Ground to be closer to family. With her relocation, John and Dianne no longer traveled five hours once a month to Spokane to care for her. Sadly, after two years, Zona passed away in March 2008. With more time on his hands, John returned to a long-time passion: model hydroplanes.

The clubs had changed a bit. A new fleet of tenth-scale electric model hydroplanes had come into being. There were new race sites and new hobby enthusiasts. Even Rose City Model Yacht Club had become a tenth-scale electric club. Almost all new hydros used fiberglass as a building material. But model hydro racing was still a hobby. John was still very much interested. He loved building the boats and decided to improve his building skills as well as racing.

When he returned to racing, Roger Newton had moved away from the RCU (Radio Control Unlimited), starting a new tenth-scale electric boat club called ERCU (Electric Radio Control Unlimited), so he joined the club and started by building his old favorite, the *Slo-mo-shun IV*, only the smaller tenth-scale model. John Howell built that first tenth-scale *Slo-mo-shun IV* for John because Howell said, "Earnest would always build them to be too heavy." They ran the new fiberglass version of *Slo-mo-shun IV*. The first time he came home from a race, Dianne noticed there was no nitro, methanol fuel odor on his clothes. She was pleased. From then on, he knew electric would be a good choice.

The boat Howell built for John, when completed, had the peaked roof effect on the bow like the eighth-scale boat Earnest had built when he first began racing. The plans were the same that John had used when he built his original *Slo-mo-shun*, only shrunk to 1/10 scale size. He felt vindicated when John Howell's new, lighter version made from the original plans, had the same unique, peak-roofed deck as when he built his *Slo-mo* back in 1974. Eventually, Roger Newton redrew the plans and made them more accurate, correcting the deck's shape.

Don Mock, curating for the Hydroplane Museum, requested models Roger Newton had designed. John offered him the *Slo-mo* that Howell built—the same boat John had raced and enjoyed. Monte Steere later gifted him a fiberglass *Slo-mo IV* molded from his own tools, which John raced for a couple of seasons.

John's comeback wasn't just about nostalgia—it marked the beginning of a deeper dive into craftsmanship and community that would lead him to one of the best builders in the field.

IMPROVING HYDRO BUILDING SKILLS

"Be the Labor Great or Small, Do It Well or Not At All"

— A favorite saying of Don Earnest, John's father

Brian Buaas, Learning Excellence in Boat Building

WHY DID THE CHICKEN CROSS THE ROAD?

BB: Only the best chickens cross the road and I am the best.

Next, John decided to again race his old favorite, *Gale V*. John met Brian Buaas through Brad Lewis. Brian and his family came to Earnest Acres about 2012. Brian agreed to help John make a new Gale mold.

There were a couple of Rose City Yacht Club meetings at Brian's house. Brian was willing to share, had great knowledge on boat building, and was a record holder for speed. At that point, the Rose City Model Yacht Club changed direction and began building and racing boats to participate with the ERCU club.

John began traveling the hour or so to Brian's house in Hillsboro for answers on how to build better boats or change the design to make them more competitive. Brian's boat building was the best of anyone around. John learned how to make molds for fiberglass boats and how to "lay up" a boat far better than he had ever done before.

MAKING A MOLD

The first step is to make a plug exactly the way the deck and bottom should look when finished. Some builders use old boats as the plug. John already had the plug for the *Gale V* made. That process requires many hours.

The plug must be solid enough to build a mold around. The plug is made from 1/16-inch plywood. Foam is added to the inside of the plug so it won't bend when fiberglass for making the mold is formed around it.

Brian showed John the steps in making a high-quality mold. He demonstrated how to use the graphite fiber and resin for the first layer. The process of laying the fiberglass over the graphite to make the mold is the next step.

Over the next several days, layers are added, allowing enough curing time between each layer so the mold does not twist or warp. The number of layers depends on the weight of the fiberglass cloth being used. This completes the laying up of the top mold for the deck.

The plug and mold must be cured for about a week before the plug may be removed from the mold and roughly cleaned up.

Now the plug is reinserted into the deck mold. The bottom of the plug is then waxed, and PVA (polyvinyl chloride), a mold release, is applied to the bottom of the plug and the sides of the deck, ready for repeating the process to make the bottom half of the mold.

The process of laying up the bottom is the same as the top deck.

When the process is completed, both molds are pulled away from the plug and the edges are cleaned up, ready to start laying up boats. The whole process takes at least 2–3 weeks and lots of time, patience, and knowledge.

After a few years, Brian exclaimed, "John, when I give building advice, you listen and use my advice! My advice usually falls on deaf ears." John now has the privilege of being the only person allowed to borrow Brian's molds.

In 2014, Brian Buaas said, "John, I'll lend you my mold if you use it to build me a boat. Would you build me an *Oh Boy! Oberto?*" John felt honored and jumped at the chance to use Brian's molds. Completed in

2015, Brian even borrowed John's *Oberto* mold, built from Brian's mold, to compete at the 2015 NAMBA Nationals Straightaway Contest. The timed, straight-line speed trials consist of racing in a straight line up and back on the race course.

"I have one requirement if you borrow this boat," John said. "When you take the boat to Nationals, put it in the Best of Scale Contest." Brian's national record speed of 69 mph won the contest. *Oberto's* run still stands as the national record for the class. And the *Oberto* also won Best of Show at the Nationals. After the exciting speed record win, John rebuilt the *Oberto* so it would be better suited for ERCU racing.

In 2015, Brian Buaas also used the *Supertest* that John had built for time trials at Lagg Lake, California. At that time, *Supertest* was officially the second fastest in the nation. That boat also won Best of Show.

Currently (2024), Brian is borrowing this mold to fashion ERCU hulls for *Miss Schweppes* and *Towne Club*. For a time, *Towne Club*, who sponsored the big hydro, had a restaurant in Portland where they served ice cream. Brian also borrowed John's classic-style mold, which John had built, to make another *Country Boy* hull. Brian is currently making the *Coors Light* and *No Name* boats.

RCU ERA
2018, *1962 DEWEY'S LUMBERVILLE DEWEY'S LUMBERVILLE,* A DISCOVERY 1/10 SCALE, ELECTRIC

Late in the 2018 season, Gentleman Jim Latimer asked John to build a *Nissan* model for him. John accepted and delivered it that fall. It was one of the last ERCU races of the season at Lacey, Washington. So John built the *Nissan* for Jim Latimer that fall. When he and Dianne went to the RCU banquet at Tri-Cities in the spring, it was fun to present Gentleman Jim with his newly completed *Nissan* and thank him for his good idea.

John was hoping to build a boat with a wooden-looking deck. Jim had told him that the *Oberto* started out with a wood deck. He said it was originally called *Miss Lumberville* in 1961 and *Dewey's Lumberville* in 1962 when they put a black cat on the tail.

He was excited about his upcoming ride in the real *Lumberville*, rebuilt and with the new name, *Oh Boy! Oberto*. During the Mahogany and Merlot event the first weekend in October on Lake Chelan in Washington State, he had a ticket to ride. David Williams from the Hydroplane and Raceboat Museum had decided to offer rides as a fundraiser for the museum.

The 1962 *Dewey's* boat sounded exciting because John had graduated from high school in 1962, and he had tried to run model boats from that year forward. He built the tenth-scale *Dewey's*. The boat's sponsor, Dewey's Lumber Company, probably did business with Copeland Lumber and so used Copeland's signature cat icon to advertise on the 1962 version that John built. The real *Lumberville* raced only two or three races between 1961 and 1962 back East. The hydroplane never did come out West. Walt Cade was one of the drivers of the boat.

Gentleman Jim had some pictures of the boat when it was *Lumberville*. Skip Young, at the museum, had more pictures. It is also a dropped-sponson boat, which is generally more stable and runs better than older hulls like *Hawaii K'ai*, with the full rounded deck. Because he had made the Supertest and the mold was the same-shaped boat, he could use that mold to build the *1962 Dewey's Lumberville*.

The boats were still made out of wood in 1962, which meant John could make a wood-looking deck. These old boats used aircraft engines from WWII airplanes. After the war, many engines were surplus and were comparatively inexpensive. So hydroplane owners began buying the engines and repurposing them for racing: Allison engines from the U.S., Rolls-Royce engines from the British.

The real *Lumberville* raced only two or three races between 1961 and 1962, changing its name to *Dewey's Lumberville* the second year. The hydroplane never did come out West.

John made his Dewey's Lumberville using fiberglass and painted a beautifully simulated wood deck. The first time John raced the Dewey's at an RCU race in Ellensburg, Washington, the contest director proclaimed, "Lumberyard won the race!" Only racing for two years in real life made it an obscure, rarely mentioned hydro in big boat history. John's boat ran well, and the model looked great.

For good measure, John built another *Lumberville* for the Hydroplane and Raceboat Museum in Kent.

EIGHTH SCALE ELECTRIC, *DEWEY'S LUMBERVILLE*

A third time, John built a *Dewey's Lumberville*. This time, he built an eighth-scale model and ran it at the same time he was racing the *Dewey's* tenth-scale. He ran the boat in 2018 and 2019.

Then COVID hit, and racing came to a halt for a few years. When racing recommenced after COVID, the boat was deemed "incorrectly" made, and though it was grandfathered in, he did not run the boat, saying it had too much of an advantage speed-wise and stability-wise compared to other boats.

Again, he was ahead of his time. Encouraged by John's experiments, several boat builders are experimenting with new ideas just like the full-sized hydroplane builders continue to do, changing the configuration of sponsons.

During COVID, 2019 and 2020, John built a tenth-scale *Dewey's Lumberville*, which he donated to the Hydroplane and Raceboat Museum in Kent. Altogether, he built three *Lumbervilles*.

CHAPTER TEN
DREAM OF A TICKET TO RIDE CHAPTER

Race at Marysville

JE: WHY DID THE CHICKEN CROSS THE ROAD?

He found out he could ride in a big hydroplane.

After the fall race at Marysville in 2015, John and Dianne sat beside Bob Senior and other boaters at the Boston Chicken restaurant to tell stories and celebrate the day's events. John began asking Bob Senior about the big hydros and knew the museum had rides. He innocently asked Bob about rides in the course of the conversation, and who rides in a real hydroplane. Was there a chance to get a ride in one? Bob smiled and replied, "I am on the board, and when they have bidding, I can get you a ride. When they run in Chelan, it's called Mahogany and Merlot." Bob explained that rides were about $1,500 and lots of fun to ride in.

On the four-hour car ride from Marysville to Battle Ground, John thought about how to get enough money for a ride. Later that week, John called the museum. It was to be a fall race, they said. It was called "Mahogany and Merlot" and was held on the first weekend in October in Chelan, Washington, on the lake. Previously, rides were given only to volunteers from the Hydroplane and Raceboat Museum. They had recently decided to open rides to the public and see if anyone would like to contribute to the museum for a ride.

Brad Lewis was at Earnest Acres when John told Brad he was going to get to ride. Dianne said, "How are you going to pay for it?" Before John could think of an answer, Brad said, "I'll buy the *Oh Boy! Oberto* and *Supertest III* from you." And John was in for a ticket to ride!

That conversation didn't just end with dinner—it sparked a journey that led John to the cockpit of some of the most iconic hydros in racing history.

2019 FIRST RIDE, Oh Boy! OBERTO
Bonus Ride With Mark Evans

When he got the money, he sent it to the museum and secured a place for a ride for the next year, 2016.

When John saw Bob again, he asked where Bob stayed when he was at Chelan. "I have always stayed at the Red Apple Inn," he said. John made reservations for the first weekend in October. Now the anticipation and excitement began.

The first weekend in October, after a four-and-a-half-hour drive up the Columbia River Gorge, over Satus Pass, they paused at Ellensburg long enough for a bite and a slow cruise past the Methodist church where they were married, the Central Washington University campus where they met, and visited Dianne's parents 'graves off the High Valley Road. When they left Ellensburg, the couple was bursting with excitement and the light, giddy feeling that comes with it. On to the Wenatchee area, famous for its apples. Turning north, John and Dianne arrived in Chelan on Friday for the ride Saturday and checked into the Red Apple Inn.

Next, they needed to visit the pits. Boats were being hoisted in and out of the water, crews were scurrying around, climbing over the boats, checking out gauges, adding fluids in various places, yelling back and forth, readying the boats for the next day.

"Hey, John." Jimmyjames Cussworth, a model boater here to enjoy the weekend, was approaching John and Dianne with his girlfriend, Teresa. When he asked if John knew who Mark Evans was, John replied, "Yes, we saw his garage last spring. He was working on his *Flip and Win* hydro when we were there." The *Flip and Win* got its name from a race.

That spontaneous ride with Mark Evans served as both a thrill and a confidence booster. The next day, John was ready.

STORY

"Mark made the hydro into a four-seater speed boat, and he is going to give us a ride. There is room for one more. You want to ride?" Dianne said, "Of course he wants to ride. Go, John, go!"

A bit later, they piled into Jimmyjames' car and went around the lake to one of the docks belonging to another motel. Mark Evans drove up with his *Flip and Win* hydroplane he had redesigned into a four-seat speed boat to meet the party, ready for a ride in *Flip and Win*. When he came back from the ride, John told Dianne that they went really fast around the hydro circuit, about 75 mph. "Mark was mostly yelling back at us and telling us all his favorite stories," very exciting. A nice introduction to fast boats!

While they were checking out the pits with boats being hoisted in and out of the water, John remembers, "I still have a grin on my face when I think of the ride. I was calm because I had gone on that ride with Mark Evans and his Flip and Win the day before." Mark Evans is a second- generation hydroplane driver, growing up and still living in Chelan. He, his brother Mitch, and father, Norm, were all past unlimited hydroplane drivers. They were well known for their driving and antics when the big hydroplanes came to town for the Apple Cup Race. There is a book, <u>Dancing With Disaster</u> by David Williams, that tells about Mark and the family, well known throughout the area for their wild ways and hydro driving skills. Mark still has a boat shop in Chelan.

John and Dianne woke up at the Apple Inn early the next day to get down to the pits soon after breakfast. At 8:00 o'clock the driver's meeting began. John was so excited he says he remembers almost nothing about the meeting except that they had one.

After the driver's meeting, Linda Williams helped John find the right size suit from a few suits available. It was an honor and thrill to be the same size as David Williams and use his suit. The suit, which drivers and riders wear, is like big mechanics 'coveralls with fireproof lining, like a fireproof jumpsuit that zips up the front over your clothes. Then a life jacket goes over that.

David's wife, Linda, helped John choose from the sizes of used suits available and fitted the helmet so it was really tight, tight enough so that the speed wouldn't lift it up and choke the wearer. The strap had to be very secure.

With a life jacket completing the outfit designed for rider's safety, John was ready in case there was a fire or in case the riders went overboard. He was suited up and ready to go. Dianne watched from the dock, a bit tense but excited for John. It was super exciting to watch the *Oh Boy! Oberto* (originally *Lumberville* in 1962) being taken to the water. The crane lifted the fully fueled and inspected boat off its trailer, into the lake, and down to the dock.

The driver was burly, 6 '5" and all of 250 pounds. Because they took the driver's seat out of the boat, there was only a board that replaced the original bench seat, still wide enough for only 1 1/2 persons. John was instructed to step into the hydro and sit down. When the driver stepped in and sat down, he was almost literally on top of John, who could not quite see around the driver or over the engine. He could see the speedometer, and they were doing 125 mph. Dianne was down on the dock. She could hear the engine speed up when the boat lurched and slid around each turn and the propeller came out of the water. The riders bounced through the corners. She could hear the sound of the rooster tail pulsing as the propeller dug in and then cleared the churned-up water. When the rooster tail stopped momentarily, the prop revved up then dug in once more, giving a rou-rou effect that could be heard across the lake. They did 3 laps. The weather was perfect with very little wind, beautiful blue sky, and the sun was out—a perfect day.

At the end of 3 laps, *Oberto* was going toward the dock but shut off too soon. They needed a tow to make it the last hundred feet to the dock. They didn't tie the boat up but had ropes to hold it to the dock. After the driver got out, the museum crew helped John out of the boat. He took his uniform off and handed the suit and helmet back to Linda. The next rider was already waiting to get suited up.

John said he was completely at ease during the ride. He remembers, "I still have a grin on my face when I think of the ride. I was calm because I had gone on that ride with Mark Evans the day before. It was that happy surprise and bonus that Jimmyjames Cussworth had invited me to ride in Mark's boat."

He was trying to take it all in. There was so much to think about. He tried to look at the gauges that were bouncing around, watching the buoys go by, water exploding up from the sponsons, a steady stream of water from the engine keeping it cool, listening to the roar of the motor.

Remembering the famous drivers that had driven that boat and the surreal feeling that he was really there watching, listening, was the thrill of a lifetime.

In 2015, John got his first ride in a full-size hydroplane. It was a reconstructed version of the *Oh Boy! Oberto*. Two years later, he rode in the reconstructed version of the 1958 *Miss Bardahl*. His third ride was the *Pay'n Pak* in the fall of 2023. *Squire Shop* is still on the bucket list because the cockpit is up in front of the engine, giving an unobstructed view of the ride.

2017, SECOND RIDE — 1958 MISS BARDAHL

On this second trip to Chelan and a second boat ride, John and Dianne decided to make a new stop. Camp Illahee was a camp that Dianne wanted to see. At the time, it was a Campfire Camp. She was the lifeguard during summer camp in 1963, the year she graduated from high school. She remembers standing at the river's edge, wearing an old beige plaid, wool coat over her bathing suit in the mornings to ward off the chill until the sun warmed the day. The camp kids used that coat in one of the evening skits, without her knowledge. During part of the skit, a camper wearing her coat ran across the makeshift stage blowing a whistle and yelling, "Everyone out of the water!", fond memories.

After the side trip down memory lane, they were off once again over Blewett Pass to Chelan, with hydro fever setting in.

The 2019 Mahogany and Merlot event was much more organized than their first experience. They stayed, again, at the Red Apple Inn with many of the boaters.

ANTIQUE MAHOGANY BOATS

This year there were also 50 or so antique mahogany boats in the slips near the pits that would form a parade and drive the full circuit around the buoys for the cheering crowd on shore to admire. How exciting for John to see his favorite wood, mahogany, used on so many boats. One of the boats had an interesting name, *Dr.'s Orders*. He asked the owner why the name. The owner said when he retired, his doctor told him he would probably be dead in a few years if he didn't get a hobby. Thus, he named his boat. He was very much alive and enjoying retirement— good advice. Many other mahogany boats filled the slips in front of the announcer's booth with spectators along the docks for viewing and photos between hydro events.

SECOND RIDE

A few months before the second ride, John was invited to be part of driver's school at the Hydroplane and Raceboat Museum in Kent, Washington. Mahogany and Merlot was now becoming more organized.

The first order of business was David Williams lecturing on the safety and aims of these rides— to be safe and have fun. After waivers were signed, eager riders were fitted with suits, and helmets. To complete the day, each rider was taken outside to one of the big hydros where they were assisted in starting up the 12-cylinder Alison engines. They were ready for Mahogany and Merlot.

In October there were friends and familiar faces as John and Dianne entered the pits, staging area for the upcoming rides.

"Do you recognize that guy?" John asked Dianne with a twinkle in his eye.

"Of course!" said Dianne. "I would recognize Chip! I remember at the Tri-Cities Columbia Cup race." That July day was sizzling hot by 11:00. Chip Hanauer was driving the Budweiser for Bernie Little. We were all sweaty. Chip looked cool, tight-jawed and suited up for the race.

"He will be a driver today?!" Dianne was impressed. Jack Shafer, past driver and now the owner of Such Crust, was there, too.

Fond memories and joy flooded back to the crowded pit area, adding to the nostalgia and joy on this perfect October day. Murmurs of "remember when" and "did you hear the story…" abounded.

John found out he would be riding in the *Miss Bardahl*. He had read David Williams 'book <u>A Race to Freedom</u> about Mira Slovak. He thought about another driver, Norm Evans, who had also driven the *Bardahl* in past races. It was with a bit of awe and trepidation that he talked about soon riding in the boat. Was he really deserving of riding in such a piece of history? One of the volunteers who helped restore the boat back at the museum reminded John that this was not really the boat those drivers used. When it was restored, only 60% or so remained. Much of the boat needed to be replaced. It put the ride more in perspective.

The wind that had come up overnight was making the water kind of rough. Testing the water had to happen to be sure the racecourse would still be OK for the upcoming rides. The turns can be especially hazardous. A driver took out one of the hydroplanes to test the water. When he came back, he gave the thumbs-up signal. And the day of rides could begin. As the perfect, warm October day progressed, the crowd on the sloping lawn and in the pits swelled until there were about three or four hundred spectators with blankets, lawn chairs, and picnic baskets, cheering and watching the festivities.

John suited up in the driver's uniform. It was when he was seated with the boat, the driver Glen beside him, that he realized he could not see over the engine to really drive safely. He decided not to try driving.

He was enjoying the ride and watching the *Pay'n Pak* speeding past their Bardahl boat on the outside. Little did he realize he would be riding in the *Pay'n Pak* a couple of years later. He could watch the hotel and shoreline pass by at a blurry, fast speed. He saw the corner buoys and more on the left and right. Some marked the outside of the course as well as the inside.

The speedometer didn't work, but the driver, Glen, said the *Bardahl* did about 125 mph and slowed down to 75 mph at the turns.

Going through the corners was exciting. The vintage boat would bounce through, skid fin and propeller lifting out of the water and then falling back into the water, giving a pulsating feeling. When they dropped back to the water, the skid fin dug in, jumping and sliding the hydro in a new direction. When the propeller came out of the water, he could hear the engine rev up, then settle back down when the propeller slammed back into the water. One second of free- wheeling makes the rou-rou-rou sound each time it hits the water again. This boat made it back to the dock without needing a tow.

It was a rough ride because of waves. He could feel the boat bounce up and down. It wasn't like he might be thrown out or the boat might tip over, but it was still bouncing erratically. The hydro slowed down at the end of the third lap, then sped up for a bonus lap! The experience this time was quite different than the first ride a couple of years earlier in the *Oh Boy! Oberto*. John completed his ride, but after a few more rides, the Bardahl broke a connecting rod and the boat was done for the day.

It was a hot day for early October with a breeze. The crowd was about 300–400 people. Additional vintage boats were in the parking lot, showing off the changes in configuration and sheer creativity of hydro builders. There were several antique boats. One, John remembers, was a long, skinny Gale.

Always taking advantage of the long trip, that year the couple bought Concord grapes to take home and can. John is also good at canning and especially loves the juice in the winter months.

2023, THIRD RIDE — PAY 'N PAK

Before heading to Chelan, John and Dianne stopped in Ellensburg to get milkshakes. As in previous trips, they went to High Valley Cemetery to see Dianne's parents 'graves. After finding the headstone and eating lunch on a nearby bench, they cleaned up the headstones and called brother Don on FaceTime to show him. He mentioned that just west of the site was where he shot his first deer.

It was fun to eat lunch at Ellensburg, where Dianne grew up and where she and John spent five years completing their degrees at Central Washington State College, now known as Central Washington University. There, too, is where John and Dianne met, fell in love, and were married.

They left Ellensburg, traveling over Blewett Pass. At the junction, they turned east toward Wenatchee on Alt. 97. After a quick stop at Mike Walker's home just outside of Cashmere, they headed north for Chelan.

Mike Walker, a retired police officer who had been a model hydroplane racer years earlier, was thinking about getting back into the sport and was happy to talk hydroplanes. They discussed possibilities of finding a model boat already ready to run. John once more was promoting the hobby he loves.

Coming into Chelan across a small bridge funneled them onto a one-way street and to the hotel entrance. Campbell's Resort Hotel has been family-owned since 1901. The crews and riders had long used this resort hotel because of its location, just steps from the pits. The hotel is on the south end of Lake Chelan, a beautiful 55-mile-long, clear, glacier-fed lake. Because it is such a deep lake, it has a beautiful, dark indigo color.

When John and Dianne checked into the hotel, a friendly, smiley girl found their name and said they were getting a special room as she handed over the key cards. The room was comfortable and had a balcony with a bird's-eye view of the pits!

After a quick walk to Safeway to pick up dinner, they ate supper overlooking the lake on their private balcony—indeed a special room. There was a view of the intimate hotel beach, two outdoor pools, and an inviting hot tub, part of the hotel grounds. Just beyond were the pits,

where there were already hydroplanes ensconced on their cribs and a crane at the ready to lift and swing boats into and out of the water. The bustle of crews gearing up for the following day and spectators milling about made anticipation of the next day even more exciting.

After supper, there was enough time to meander down to the pits and watch David Williams roll out one of the four barrels of airplane fuel and put it in place for the next days of rides. As the barrels emptied, they would be trucked to the local airport and refilled. This happened several times throughout the weekend. Crews were setting up the boats ready to run the next day. Old model hydroplane friends Gale Whitestein and Rocky Freidel said hello as well. Linda, David's wife, was there organizing the next day of rides.

Quiet excitement was mounting. Eight carefully rebuilt hydroplanes with Allison or Rolls-Royce engines, a crane, suits on hangers, new helmets taken out of boxes, life jackets in place, chairs, sign-up tent with the paperwork, and many more necessities in place ready for the weekend— quite a change from the ride two years ago. 1958 *Miss Bardahl, Miss Wahoo, 1948 My Sweetie* (for show, did not give rides), *1972 Pay 'n Pak, Bluechip, Notre Dame* (repainted from *Oh Boy! Oberto*), Tahoe Miss, and Miss Thriftway were crowded into the small pit area, preparing for the weekend activities.

Following a light breakfast of comfort food—Cheerios, raisin toast, and a banana in the motel room—it was down to the pits by 8:00. The *Pay 'n Pak* was running some warm-up laps.

Driver's meeting was at 9:00. They went over the rules for the rides: be safe, have fun. As the ride finishes, get out of the life jacket, helmet, and suit and clear off the dock as soon as possible so that the next ride can be suited up. David made sure to explain the hand signals to the driver since it is too loud to talk over the engine during the ride. John's instructions were: thumbs up means keep going, thumbs down means there is a problem—slow down, trouble with your helmet, can't see.

All boats are connected to the race coordinator using a screen connected to the dashboard. A green light meant you are clear to keep going. Yellow light, slow down and return to the pits with caution. Red means stop, turn off the engine, wait for instructions.

"Do not go near the alcohol booth in the parking lot," said David Williams. "If you even walk into the bar, do not come back to the pit area for the rest of the day. Alcohol and anyone who has imbibed is strictly forbidden in the pits."

Another safety precaution: "Only the rider and one friend (spouse) can be on the dock when you get your ride." The limited dock area gets crowded.

David said he would try to assign the boat the riders requested, but not to be disappointed if it didn't work out. "Boats break down, but we will do our best. We want you to have fun and make your day special," was the major goal. And true to their word, the museum crew went above and beyond. The day was special, always to be remembered.

There were GoPro cameras mounted on the boat—one on the middle of the tail wing looking forward, another on the dashboard to the right of the driver looking back at both of the riders and the rooster tail. Take-home videos of each ride were available for each rider afterward.

Suiting up is more sophisticated now with new suits, life jackets, and helmets purchased for Mahogany and Merlot and other events. Racks of suits, life jackets, and new helmets became the dressing room. Riders signed in with Linda at the sign-up table in order to get a ride.

John and Dianne saw the *Pay'n Pak* running, and it was clearly faster than any of the other boats they had seen run. John was helped into a driving suit and life jacket by two capable ladies. He tried on the helmet and it fit. They had him wiggle his head from side to side to test the fit—and it fit very well. He gave up his cochlear implants to save them from getting damaged. He could still feel the roar of the engine and is pretty sure he could hear it. What he did not realize was how tight the chin strap needed to be until the hydro was in the backstretch.

Linda Williams had always said that the helmet would lift up. if it was not snug enough. It didn't on the first two rides, so he was not concerned about it. To his surprise, he found out that it did lift up with the fast *Pay'n Pak* ride.

Dianne and John were ushered down to the dock, where the ride ahead of him was coming in. They helped John into the boat and showed him how to hang on to the barn handle bolted behind the driver with his right hand. He sat beside the driver on the left side and a bit back from the driver's seat. He got into the boat and Driver Dan joined him on the right side, and they were ready.

He gave Dan thumbs up and they pushed away from the dock. The primer began to buzz, the boat coughed and quit. Then with some more primer and starter, they were off.

The rest was kind of a blur. At the speed they drove, the force to remain in his seat, hang onto the barn door handle with one hand and the side of the cowling with the other to keep from sliding around, kept John busy.

John remembers, "We went down the backstretch and the helmet began to lift. My left hand had to hang on to the helmet, and the right hand gripped the barn handle. The boat went much faster than either the *Miss Bardahl* or the *Oh Boy! Oberto*."

They came to the first corner at full speed. The more modern pickle fork *Pay'n Pak* did not need to slow down like the old round-nose hydros did. The other boats had to slow down and bounce through the corner. The *Pay'n Pak* didn't change motor RPMs around the corners and down the front stretch. All were at the same speed, a steady rooster tail fountain of water in the wake.

When they came to the right-hand turn again, there was so much force at that speed that John gripped hard on the handle as he slid around. It caught him by surprise. Then down the backstretch they went, hand holding on to his helmet again. There wasn't time to sit back and watch the surroundings like he did in the *Bardahl*.

Going through the corners was almost twice as fast. Going through the turns was a whole different experience. Same going down the back and front stretches. He had to enjoy the feel of the ride, its forces, and hold on tight. The speedometer was broken, so he had to rely on the driver to tell him the speed after the ride. They went around three times, slowed down, then sped up—and John got an extra lap!

When the hydro came in, John exited the boat. Linda wanted the helmet and life jacket immediately. He took off the red driver's suit back in the pits. The pit boss said the speed was about 135–140 mph. Later, John was interviewed by the radio announcer up at the patio about his three rides. In his interview, they were asking which boat he liked best. He explained each boat was so different that they were all a thrill. Afterward, he helped sell tickets at the entrance to the pit area. Many stopped to ask him questions and listen as he expounded upon his tale of the rides. It was a special treat for John to tell about his experience and good public relations for those who might want to sign up for rides.

From his very first ride in the *Oh Boy! Oberto* to the vintage charm of the *Miss Bardahl* and the modern thrill of the *Pay 'n Pak*, John's hydroplane experiences have been a journey of adrenaline, nostalgia, and heartfelt memories. Each ride not only brought a new level of excitement but also deepened his connection to a community united by passion for speed and the water. As John reflects on these moments, he is reminded that every journey—whether fast or nostalgic—adds another layer to a life filled with adventure.

LESSONS LEARNED: LEGACY
Be kind, make friends, help when you can.

Do your best.

Pay attention to input from others; learn from others. Increase your skills.

Try new ideas.

Priorities: Remember what is most important; the way one lives needs to reflect that. Fiercely compete in your own way.

From his beginnings and throughout his life, John has maintained a thread of basic ideas in his approach to living. Being kind, having integrity, being a fierce competitor, always learning and experimenting, and reaching out in friendly ways is his mantra.

He often surprises people he meets because of his positive attitude about any situation. John believes there are better ways to solve problems than getting angry. He loves meeting and talking with people about boats or old cars. On subjects that interest him most, he not only joins clubs and organizations—he becomes involved in some way: as a leader, an officer, or simply by showing up at meetings and events.

He shares the love of his hobbies with whomever he meets. Many hobbyists have spent hours in his shop or car barn, learning gems of knowledge which he offers freely.

He will be remembered for his willingness to share his vast knowledge and his friendly approach to living. His philosophy is summed up by his favorite saying:

"Be the labor great or small, do it well or not at all."

END NOTES

People Who Have Helped John Throughout the Years

With His Model Hydroplane Hobby and Assisted Dianne in Writing This Book

Patrick Brown – A writer who took the time to gently and thoroughly read through the early drafts of this book. He offered helpful suggestions on how to proceed.

Brian Buass – A national record holder for speed who helped John learn how to make proper molds for building hydroplanes. Brian borrowed two of John's boats—*Oh Boy! Oberto* and *Miss Supertest*—to set those records.

Dennis Caines – Thank you for making the effort and allowing us to use your splendid photos— not just of John's boats, but of many years of racing seasons.

Harry Collier (MV) – John's college roommate and best man at his wedding, Harry helped rekindle John's interest in model hydroplanes. In the 1970s, Harry built *Miss Seattle* while John built *Slo-mo-shun IV*, and he assisted in the construction of that first boat. Harry passed away in 1996, marking the end of a treasured friendship.

Dallas Cook – Always full of stories and commentary that kept race days fun. He raced in the 1980s and shared a treasure trove of hydro racing programs, newsletters, stats, and photos. His humorous take— always calling the boats "toy boats"—reminded everyone it was a hobby and meant to be fun.

Ron Daum – One of the charter members of RCU who has raced with John since before 1976. He helped write the original half-page of rules, and the many that followed. He remains active in racing as of 2025.

John Howell – A racing buddy who began building boats with John around 1982. They traveled to many races together. His upbeat attitude and focus on lightweight boats have made the hobby more enjoyable.

Don Goetschius – John's brother-in-law and a constant source of encouragement. Don often visited the house to check on the latest happenings—whether piano lessons or boat builds in the basement. Even after he could no longer attend races, he continued to support John's efforts, and his wife, Nancy, brought him to races when possible. Don passed away, but his influence lives on.

Ezra Kidowski – An accomplished writer who encouraged Dianne and wrote a book report for the website.

Kerry Kjos – Served on the ERCU board with John. They traveled to many races and spent long hours building boats together in John's workshop. He is still actively racing.

Brad Lewis – An enthusiastic boater with a vast knowledge of hydroplane history. He has shared memorabilia, offered expert advice, and helped John make his boats more historically accurate.

Howard Price – A retired Boeing machinist who crafted many of the intricate metal parts for John's boats, including the fifth-scale *Gale V*. His tiny, authentic replicas contributed to several of John's "Best of Show" awards. Howard raced until he passed away.

Roger Newton – A pioneer in the model hydroplane world, Roger sold plans still used today and helped form many of the clubs. Known as "The Czar," he mentored countless racers and worked on full-size boats at the Hydroplane and Race Boat Museum.

Norm Nordby – Owner of Hobbies Unlimited in Portland and longtime Commodore of the Rose City Model Yacht Club when John joined in 1974. He raced model hydroplanes and contributed to the club's legacy.

Les Ruggles – An early boat designer and builder, Les was instrumental in founding model hydroplane clubs alongside Ron Daum and Harry Collier. He taught John how to attach sponsons correctly and raced through the 1970s and '80s. He passed away many years ago.

David Williams – Promoter and overseer of the Hydroplane and Race Boat Museum in Seattle, Washington. David is always willing to answer questions and has written several outstanding books referenced in this one.

Skip Young – The retired editor of *[Publication Named "HYDRO RAVE!"]*. John and Dianne often see him at the museum, and his deep knowledge of racing history has made John's model boats more accurate. Skip has shared many stories about the races of years past.

ATLAS VAN LINES

COE-Z-MISS

EVERGREEN – ROOFING

MISS HOUSTON

MISS THRIFTWAY

SAVAIR'S MIST

SAVAIR'S MIST

STATISTICS

POINTS AND PLACEMENT

John has always been interested in keeping track of his points. His fascination with numbers and fierce desire to compete have inspired this section. It all began when he was a kid attending the Spokane Indians baseball games. He liked to write down the play-by-play statistics. Then, as a baseball manager throughout college, he kept statistics and reported them weekly to the local newspaper. He has kept track of his hydroplane hobby points from the beginning.

NITRO ERA

1999 RCU – John was inducted into the Hall of Fame for driver points with over 150,000 points. 162,833 accumulated points in Nitro.

2016 – ERCU was inducted into the Hall of Fame.

In the 1980s he placed well with driver points and was recognized for best built boats. Here's the list and his points placement against other boats:

1986 = 4th place 1987 = 7th place 1988 = 2nd place 1989 = 9th place

2023 = 12th in RCU driver points – 300,000+ 5th in ERCU driver point standing

Gale V – Best of Scale four times: 2018, 2019 RCU 1/8th scale POINTS ACCRUED THROUGHOUT THE YEARS

Fast Electric boats – 11,171 points 1/10th scale – no points kept

ERCU vintage – 1962 Gale V with 5,965 points is presently seventh place compared to all ERCU boats ever run.

1/10th scale vintage boat – 67,576 points 1/10th scale modern hub – 4,573 points Driver points up to 2023 season – 75,231

2016 – Inducted into the RCU Hall of Fame

BOATS THAT JOHN BUILT

John was and is a prolific boat builder. Using his knowledge and attention to detail and excellence in performance, a list of boats he built or helped to build was a must.

FIRST ROUND OF BOATS – 1/8 SCALE, NITRO, WOOD-BUILT 1976–1992

1. *Slo-mo-shun* IV in Spokane – 9th or 10th grade

2. Miss Thriftway in Spokane – 10th grade

3. Miss Thriftway Too in Spokane – 11th grade

4. Tiger – 11th grade, created his own hydro

5. *Slo-mo-shun* IV – built 1976–1978, ran the boat in 1977 Rookie of the Year

6. 1956–57 version Miss Wayne – built in 1977, ran the boat in 1977

7. 1958 Gale V – built in 1978, ran the boat in 1978–1979

8. A boat for John Montgomery

9. 1971 Country Boy – ran the boat in 1981

10. Supertest III – ran the boat

11. Les Ruggles started the boat – 1/8 nitro

12. 1962 Gale V – ran the boat in 1986

13. 1988 Budweiser

14. 1991 & 1992 Gale VII – 1/10 scale electric, wood, ran the boat in 1991 and 1992

Best of Scale 3 times

ELECTRIC ERA AND FIBERGLASS ERA 1992–present

Boats for John Howell

1. Miss Radio Graphics

2. Sony Jim Jam – 1/10 scale

3. Purple Savair's Mist – 1/10 scale

4. 1963 Tahoe Miss – helped build for John Howell

5. 1950 Slo-mo-shun IV – 1/10 scale wood 1950 Slo-mo-shun IV – 1/10 scale fiberglass

6. Gale's 1965 Roostertail – 1/10 scale, made for Howard Price

7. 1978 Supertest – 1/10 scale

8. 1962 Gale V – 1/10 scale

9. 1960 Miss Thriftway – 1/10 scale, helped Kerry Kjos make

10. 2013 *Oh Boy! Oberto* – 1/10 scale, speed record holder

11. 2013 Second Oh Boy! Oberto Boats for Brad Lewis

12. Dayton Walther – 1/8 nitro

13. Dayton Walther – 1/10 electric *Boats for Chuck Murray*

14. Nitrogen Too – 1/10

15. Olympia Beer – 1/10

16. Olympia Beer – 1/8 Hull to replace Miss Houston

17. Savair's Mist (pink) – 1/10 scale Has become Coe-Z-Miss Boats for Rick Evans

18. Notre Dame – 1/10 scale, 2018

19. Redman II – 1/10 scale, 2019

20. Evergreen Roofing – 1/10 scale, 2020

21. Pay 'n Pak – 1/10 scale, 2020

22. 1962 Dewey's Lumberville – 1/10 scale, 2018

23. 1962 Dewey's Lumberville – 1/10 scale *Sample for Hydroplane Museum, 2018*

He then built and ran a 1/8 scale 1962 Dewey's Lumberville at the same time that he ran the 1/10th scale 1962 Dewey's Lumberville. He also built a replica that he donated to the Raceboat and Hydroplane Museum.

1. 1962 Dewey's Lumberville – 1/8 scale, 2019

2. U-33 Nissan – built for Jim Latimer, 1/10 scale, 2019

3. Boat for Kevin from Wisconsin – Olympia Beer, 1/10 scale
All finished except the paint

4. Slo-mo-shun IV – 1/8 scale Donated to the Hydroplane Museum

5. Gale V – 1/5 scale Donated to the Hydroplane Museum (gas)

6. Gale's Roostertail – for Paxton Renunen (hull only)

7. Island Securities – hull only

8. Atlas Van Lines – for Tom Markos, helped to build

9. Hawaii Kai 1957 – for David Newton

10. Hawaii Kai 1955 – for Chuck Murray

11. Mark and Pak – (hull by Brian Buass), John completed

12. 1960 Miss Thriftway – for Rick Evans 1957 Wood Grain Thriftway Too – for Ron Daum, in process John has also patched up, rebuilt, and repainted many boats.

HONORS AND AWARDS BEST OF SCALE

The following is a list of hydroplanes for which John received Best of Scale honors:

Eighth Scale Nitro

- Gale V

- 1984 Columbia Cup

- 1985 Columbia Cup

- 1988 Silver Cup

- 1989 Columbia Cup

- Gale VII
- 1991 Diamond Cup
- 1992 Columbia Cup
- 1992 Silver Cup
- 1992 Gold Cup
- Budweiser
- 1989 Bill Muncey Memorial Cup
- 1995 Chenoweth Cup
- 1996 Gold Cup

Tenth Scale Electric

- Gale V
- 2007 Woodland
- 2008 Woodland
- 2014 Roger Newton Memorial Cup
- 2015 Roger Newton Memorial Cup
- 2015 *Oh Boy! Oberto* – won Lagg Lake National Straightaway Speed Record for modern boat class and Best of Show

Driver: Brian Buass

- 2015 Supertest – Lagg Lake National Straightaway Speed Record for vintage boat class and Best of Scale
- *Driver: Brian Buass*